The Golden Spider

Dan Liberthson

ACKNOWLEDGMENTS

I am grateful to Kathy Rawlins for her steadfast help
and support and, for their valuable suggestions, to
Joe Kornfeld, Judy Windt, Nancy Etchemendy, Custis Haynes,
Nancy Faass, Andrea Stryer, and Adin Gilman-Cohen.

This book is dedicated to the memory of Susan Eastwood.

Cover art and design are by Julie Weaver.

Published by Fennel Press, San Francisco, CA
ISBN: 1475195486
ISBN-13: 978-1475195484

CONTENTS

1 SOMETHING'S WRONG

"Why would they attack again so soon?" the tallest and youngest of the three Guardians asked, baffled but insistent. "They caused such destruction and misery not so long ago, you'd think even *they* would be satisfied." His face contracted and he stared wildly into space for a moment during which his companions shared in the vision of slaughter that seized his mind. Bodies exploded amid shrieking missiles, wounded children wandered blindly, too stunned even to whimper, and firestorms swept through homes and forests.

A lone collie gazed mournfully from high on a boulder and loosed a despairing howl at the smoke-smeared moon. And behind it all a grotesque silhouette stalked, like a huge shadow congealed to a solid, horrible thing. Mocking laughter issued from this beast, so low and powerful it was more felt than heard, deeply felt, like the dense beat of enormous taiko drums.

The young Guardian hid his face in the crook of his arm, rubbing for comfort against his soft wool sleeve. He squeezed his eyes shut as if to blind himself to his own painful memory. Then he dropped his arm, lifted his head, and pleaded, not to any in his company but to someone or something unseen. "Surely this cannot happen again? Not here, not in this time when we have grown so much and come so far!"

As the three resumed walking, a knife-edged silence sliced between them and the evening sunlight stretched their shadows bowstring tight on the path. The stocky, gray-haired woman in the center turned, grasped the young man around the biceps, and brought him to a stop. She looked directly

1

into his eyes as she spoke, head tilted back to cope with his height, blunt features gripping his attention like a vice.

"Has the Council of Guardians taught you nothing, Simon? Are you so naive as to think that *time* has meaning for the Dark Ones? Short time, long time—they don't live in time, they have nothing to do with it. When you have survived as long as I have, you will know. They invade when there is opportunity, when there is invitation. And even if we human beings have grown, we go on inviting them."

The third Guardian in the group, who had plodded on a few paces after the others stopped, turned back and joined them. He was the oldest, his broad forehead deeply creased and his face webbed by wrinkles, but he stood straight, nearly as tall as the younger man, and spoke firmly.

"The Council issued a warning, but its import has yet to unfold. This may not be a serious incursion, but merely a feint to draw our attention while the main attack overwhelms some other world. If this is true, the Great Book may show it."

He stroked his broad white beard and then ran the fingers of both hands through the fringe of white hair that ringed his bald head like froth around a worn rock. Finally, he nodded as if he'd made an important decision.

"Yes, I must return home to consult *The Book of Life.* Whether this challenge is major or of no great concern, we may then know, and we will meet again to plan accordingly."

With each hand, he took and held the hands of his two companions, studying their faces in turn. Then he smiled, gave their hands a little squeeze, and walked away with a steady tread. Turning a last time, he said "Go in gladness but keep the watch," his smile broadening as if to brighten them all.

Yet by the time he emerged from the park, the old Guardian's show of calm for his companions' sake had been shaken. He walked urgently, anxiously, as if impelled by a jagged inner force barely contained. He was thinking of his grandson, whom he had hoped would live in a time of peace, never to face chaos and destruction.

"He is still too young, not nearly ready," the old man muttered as he forced his legs to climb the stairs to his apartment building. "If Jeremy cannot escape war, then at least grant him time to find himself before he must fight," he prayed, though he did not know to whom. With a hiss of impatience, he fumbled at his keys, trying the wrong one and nearly breaking it off in the lock before he realized his mistake and managed to open the door.

As he climbed more stairs to his apartment, his breath grew ragged, and he tried to calm himself by remembering pleasant hours spent there with his grandson, side by side immersed in ancient history. Nearly gasping, he wrenched open the door and dropped quickly and gratefully into a large leather chair facing a roll-top desk piled with books and papers.

He took a deep breath and reached for a thick old volume bound in worn dark leather. No title graced the cover, but it was inlaid with beautiful golden designs of plants and animals twined around a human couple clasping hands. His gnarled fingers leafed through pages of pictures painted in vivid colors and pages of exotic script, its elegant whorls and slashing diagonals flowing with a visual rhythm that evoked a symphony.

The old man let himself sink back in his chair and massaged his deeply crevassed forehead, grimacing as if in pain. "So far, nothing," he murmured to himself, heaving a sigh that ended with a flutter of the lips sounding like a small motor. His breath stirred the curly hair of his full, long beard and lifted the dipping ends of his moustache. "But the High Council of Guardians does not cry wolf. There must be some basis for their warning."

For a long while, he sat and caressed his head, knitting his sprouting white eyebrows, intense with thought. Then he pulled a large briar pipe from his jacket pocket, filled it with tobacco from a tin in the top desk drawer, and lit it with a wooden kitchen match.

"Always best to be thorough," he muttered, turning again to the untitled book. "Too much depends on it." Puffing on his pipe until he sat beneath an umbrella of smoke, he leafed through page after page, examining each closely, bunching his eyebrows and furrowing his forehead.

Outside, a thunderstorm began, and in the lightning's flicker the pictures in the book came alive. Scenes of ancient times rose and passed: kings and queens clothed in splendor, powerful athletes grappling for the wreath of victory. Farmers planted in Spring, harvested in Fall, and held joyful festivals of thanksgiving to the river that fed their land. A priest leading a procession cut the throat of a white bull and offered the blood, caught in a silver basin, to the statue of a god with many faces.

Time passed as the pages turned, until modern scenes unfolded, of factory and farm, city and town, land and sea. Worshippers still held processions, but now they wound through paved or cobblestone streets to churches, temples, and mosques. Seasons changed, rain fell, snow whirled, dark fell and froze, and sunlight washed over the lands again.

At last, the old Guardian's thick fingers hovered over a picture of graceful, smiling people wearing richly decorated robes, chatting and relaxing in a flower garden. He frowned as he studied the scene. Something was wrong. And there it was, there! A blot of red had appeared at the top of the page. It crept down like a thin river of blood, shaping itself as it crawled.

The old man's broad trunk stiffened with revulsion, and he groaned as the air was forced from his lungs. "They *are* here," he cried in dismay, rising to his feet and bracing straight-armed over the book. "The warning was just in time." Through the picture thrashed a malevolent red worm, lashing out as if to burst from the page.

4

The people in the picture no longer talked and laughed and smiled. Faces twisting with hate, they threw themselves at one another, screaming and tearing like mad beasts. The old man drew back, his eyes widening with shock. Then he pushed away from the desk and staggered back against a bookcase that filled the entire rear wall of his apartment. There he clung as books tumbled down around him.

For the last time, strength flared up in his body. His lips moved, and with a faint but steady voice he began to chant in a strange, melodious language. He raised his right arm and swept it across the room until it pointed, palm forward, at the book. As his chant ended, he held this position, like a sorcerer sealing a spell. The red worm at first faded, but then pulsed stubbornly, malignantly, as if insisting on the last word.

A powerful shudder shook the old man. His arm fell to his side, his knees buckled, and he sank into a squat, still leaning back against the bookcase. For a moment he tried to rise, straining as if against enormous weight, but his legs refused to lift him. Utterly spent, he slumped sideways and sank to the floor.

His lips moved slowly, with profound effort. "I am done, yes, but there *is* hope for the boy," he whispered, as if someone must be listening. Then his eyes closed, his breath left, and he was still. But in the open book upon the desk the worm no longer writhed and the red mark faded slowly from sight.

2 WHAT JUST HAPPENED?

"Man," Jeremy Taylor called to his friend Zack, "you'd be worse than Frankenstein if they let you have a real lab."

Jeremy and Sandy, Zack's sister, left the doorway and entered Zack's room, which really did look like the lair of a mad scientist. The bookcase was crammed to overflowing with biology, math, astronomy, and computer programming books. Tools, electronic equipment, partly finished models, printout, and piles of scribbled note paper littered the floor. Jeremy and Sandy had to pick their way carefully to a battered wooden table where Zack stood at the microscope poking up from the wreckage of a chemistry set.

"Don't bump Tyranno-man," Zack warned. "His glue's not dry yet."

"He's totally gruesome," Sandy said, grinning wolfishly. "Could you sic him on Tina Warren, the jerk who tried to knock me over in P. E.?"

"He's not done yet," Zack said. "I wrecked the arms. Anyway, I'm tired of these crummy models. I wish I could do real bioengineering."

"Yeh, terrific," Jeremy grinned. "You'd create some evil super-organism that would wipe out most of mankind."

"And I'd program it to eat you first," Zack quipped, returning the grin. "One piece at a time. But I won't get the chance anytime soon." His smile slumped, but then brightened again. "Hey!" he blurted, "I got some water from that scummy pond behind the school. It should have really neat stuff—let's check it out. Maybe we'll find . . . the Creature from the Green Slime!"

Zack twisted his face into a slobbering monster's and groped at Sandy, who slapped his hands away. "You're no great scientist, Zack—just a disgusting human being," she giggled. "Something's wrong with your genes."

"Then yours have to be messed up too," Zack shot back.

"You're both incredibly weird" Jeremy said, shaking his head and grinning.

Zack ignored him, dug an eyedropper out of the mess on the table, and sucked up some pond water. Holding his tongue between his teeth, he let a small drop fall on a blank slide. "Here goes nothing," he muttered dramatically, flourishing a thin glass slip-cover, placing it over the liquid, and finally clipping the slide into the microscope. "Let's see what we've got, sports fans."

Zack bent over the scope and twisted the focus knob. Sandy and Jeremy stared at the back of his head, as if they could see through his eyes. Then they both realized at once how silly they looked, and started giggling and bumping shoulders. Jeremy felt himself begin to blush, so he glanced away out the window.

The grass was rippling under a rising wind, and toward the horizon thunderheads piled up, rumbling black against the gray-blue sky. Jeremy couldn't have said why, but he felt an anxious sensation crawling from the pit of his stomach and spreading. He shuddered, suddenly chilled even in the warm, stuffy room.

"Nothing outstanding, folks," Zack said, with a tsk of disgust and a sigh. "Just plain old Paramecia."

"Para-what?" Sandy asked, tittering nervously.

"Parachutes," Jeremy answered, as the jittery sensation retreated and he felt almost normal again. "Little guys with parachutes."

"Quit it," Zack yelled. "I showed you a picture yesterday—they've got those tiny beating hairs called cilia? And there are euglenas too, the ones with the long tails that whip around."

"Flagella," Jeremy murmured. "The long tails are flagella."

"Like spaghetti" Sandy said. "All they need is sauce and meatballs."

"Be serious, Sandy," Zack ordered, "or you won't get to look. Wait! There's a Stentor in there! It's got this big opening with cilia beating all around to drag in the little guys. Check it out!"

Jeremy shoved Zack aside and put his eye to the scope. "There it is!" he shouted, adjusting the focus knob. "It looks like a big tuba. Wow, it just gobbled a Paramecium and now it's after seconds. That is soooo cool. Watch out, little guys!"

"Whoa!" he suddenly shouted, grabbing the scope's barrel. "Where'd that other thing come from? Zack, there's a red, twisty thing sucking in everybody else. Holy smoke! It just got the Stentor!"

"Impossible!" Zack yelled, tugging Jeremy's arm. "Stentor's king of the hill! Let me see."

"It's my turn!" Sandy snapped, shoving between them. "I see it—a wiggly red worm with a zillion legs and claws. Wait! Zack, it's growing!"

Sandy's voice squeaked with surprise and she backed away from the microscope so fast she bumped into her brother.

"Hey," Zack said, grinning and cocking his head. "You guys are messing with me, right? I'll bet there's nothing." He pushed Sandy aside and put his eye to the scope. "Incredible!" he said, whistling softly. "You're *not* kidding. I've never seen that, even in books. It looks like a millipede crossed with a scorpion, but there's this gullet with rotating cilia, like blades. It shreds its prey and then sucks in the scraps. That thing is going bananas—it's cleaning out the whole drop!

"Oh, man," he muttered to himself, "I've got to tell somebody about this. I could be famous—but I'll have to have evidence!" He glanced quickly at Jeremy and snapped "grab my camera," pointing to where it lay in a corner. "Quick!"

"Come on, Zack," Sandy urged as Jeremy reached for the camera. "Tell us what that is. You know just about everything!"

8

"Not this," Zack muttered, putting his eye to the scope again. "Wait a minute. It's gone!" he nearly yelled, scanning the slide in a panic. "Where are you? Come on!" At last his shoulders slumped and, holding back tears, he turned to Jeremy and Sandy. "It was swallowing everything, this fantastic new species, but it's gone. Nobody will believe me now."

"It has to be in there," Sandy said, taking the scope and peering down. "I saw it first, don't forget. I'll bet I can find it again." She scrolled across the droplet, her forehead and nose wrinkled with concentration. "You're right, Zack," she admitted, looking up at her brother. "There's nothing in there now. No little bugs, no creepy-crawly. Are you sure your scope's okay?"

Zack stiffened and glared at her. He looked like somebody who, even though he couldn't swim and feared heights, found himself at the end of the ten-meter board, his common sense telling him not to jump but something else making him go where he knew he shouldn't. And then he plunged.

"Yes, dammit!" he snarled, with a meanness neither Jeremy nor Sandy had ever heard from him before. "You assholes both saw that thing before I did. If my microscope's wrecked, then you did it!"

"*We* wrecked it?" Sandy shot back, her eyes widening. "*We* didn't hurt your precious microscope and *you* are taking your itty-bitty experiments way too seriously. Take it back and say you're sorry, Zack."

"You don't know anything about science and you never will," Zack snapped, his eyes blazing. "Both of you can go to hell!"

Sandy and Jeremy stood gaping as if Zack had slapped them, until she broke the silence. "Screw you, Zack!" she yelled. "You are becoming a total turd! Come on, Jeremy, let's get out of here. We're better off throwing a football around than trying to talk to my jerk brother."

Rushing down the hall, the two friends stumbled over Charley, Zack's fat old golden retriever. The dog heaved himself up and plodded over, wagging his whole hind end in greeting. "That's a good boy," Jeremy murmured, scratching behind Charley's ears.

He needed time to think, and took some deep breaths to stop feeling like he'd been punched in the gut. Zack was supposed to be his best friend—they'd stuck together ever since moving onto the same suburban block—but Zack had just spat hate at him.

Jeremy scoured his memory but couldn't find anything to explain it. Zack was a weedy kid with dirty-blond hair that fell over coke-bottle eyeglasses without which he was nearly blind. He could be pushy, trying to make you learn something or admit he was right, but that was just stubbornness—he'd always been basically nice. He was terrible at sports, but not a bad loser—and he didn't rub it in when he won, which he usually did at mental games like chess.

Sandy called Zack "the Wiz" because he had a genius IQ. He liked to be left alone to peer through his telescope or microscope, mess with his chemistry set, search the Web, program on his computer, or soak up every entry in dictionaries and encyclopedias with his photographic memory. But he was always friendly too, and had a goofball sense of humor. Zack had never seemed to have a mean bone in his body, yet he'd just hit them with pure nastiness. Why?

"Sandy," Jeremy said, "do you have any idea what just happened? One minute Zack was cool, and the next minute he bit our heads off. I don't get it."

"Me neither," Sandy replied in a tense voice. "Zack's been like a grenade lately. Something pulls his pin, you never know what, and then, watch out!"

Thoroughly rubbing Charley's sides, Jeremy didn't look at Sandy—he was afraid she'd see that he was ashamed of letting her take charge instead of standing up to Zack himself. Sandy didn't take crap from anybody, Jeremy thought admiringly, but he'd never be that tough no matter how hard he tried.

10

The problem was that Zack's vicious, false accusation had made him really mad. And when Jeremy got really, really mad, instead of springing into action he went weak and started trembling inside. Because of this, he'd never been any good at fights or arguments, and he tried to hide the problem by avoiding tense situations. After all, what if Zack got so crazy he started something?

Was I scared more than surprised? Jeremy asked himself. Yes, he answered. He hated it, but he definitely was a chicken. At least Sandy hadn't figured this out, he hoped—she'd been too angry herself and too busy thinking of a good come-back for Zack.

"Come on," Sandy said, rousing from her own silent funk and again taking command of the situation. "Let's get out of here. I don't want to be anywhere near Zack right now." They ran downstairs and the old dog followed them, but when they trotted off toward the field he gave up and lay down in his favorite sunny spot on the porch.

It was a Saturday morning in early October, warm in the sunlight though cold breezes foretold the harsh Midwestern winter. The leaves had already turned colors and the wind skittered those that had fallen. For a while, the friends passed and kicked the football around, but neither really felt like playing.

The sky was blue overhead, but lightning flashed in the dark gang of clouds gathering toward the horizon. The zigzag glare reminded Jeremy of the red, writhing thing they'd seen in the pond water. He felt himself tense up and decided to think of something else.

"Down and out fifteen yards," he yelled at Sandy, and then threw a bullet pass a little behind her, but she spun and snatched it in.

"All right!" she shouted, tossing the ball back to Jeremy. "Sandy makes the tough grab for first down yardage!"

Straw-blond, stocky, and bossy in a nice way, Sandy seemed to Jeremy more like a thirteen-year-old boy than a girl a few months over twelve. She wanted to be the first female professional football player—a tight end or a wide receiver—and she made Zack play quarterback even though his wobbly throws often fell short. Her gawky brother was a year younger, eight inches taller, and far less coordinated, sometimes tripping over himself as he fell back from center to pass.

Jeremy was smaller and even skinnier than Zack, but he could run and turn quicker and had a far better arm. Sandy liked him because he could put a rock into a tree hole from twenty yards.

"I can't figure out what's eating Zack," Sandy said as they walked home. "I wish I could. He's usually pretty nice—like after I told him your sister Sara was sick, he asked all about it and tried to figure out ways to help. But he gets so intense. He wants to be a famous scientist and sometimes he thinks everybody's trying to hold him back, like Dad and his teachers. Whenever he thinks he won't make it, he needs to blame somebody, and since Mom left he's been getting worse."

Sandy mused a bit, tossing up the football underhanded and catching it as they walked. Then she stopped and turned to Jeremy. "What do you think about that weird thing in the pond water?" she asked anxiously. "Why did it show up in that one drop, almost like it was there just for Zack, but then we saw it too? And how did it just disappear?"

"I don't know," Jeremy said, shrugging to hide how much he too was spooked. He didn't want Sandy to think he was gutless enough to be scared, but he had the same feeling she did, that somehow the thing on the slide had come for Zack and by chance found all of them. "Creature from the Green Slime," he shrugged with a short, barking laugh, twisting his face to imitate a monster, just as Zack had. Then he looked straight at Sandy and tried to keep his voice steady.

"Seriously though, I'll bet there was a red thread or a hair caught in the eyepiece. That happened to me in Bio lab. Better tell Zack to try some lens paper before he announces his discovery to the world."

"Yeh, that could be it," Sandy said softly, not really convinced but with no better theory. Then the two friends walked on in silence, watching the storm gather. Though they both needed an answer, neither of them could really believe Jeremy's explanation. The thing had to be real. It was too ugly for anything else, and it was devouring everything.

"Jeremy," Sandy asked as they came to their block, "how is Sara?"

"No better," Jeremy answered. "Aunt Lillian took care of her yesterday so Mom and Dad could have a break. They're pretending everything will be okay, but they're really worried, I can tell."

"She's such a neat kid, Jer! Everybody likes her. Geez, you'd think that with your dad being a doctor and your mom a teacher they could figure it out. But there's other weird stuff happening. Last night the TV went on before I even touched it. I told Dad but he thought I was joking. If something's not on his computer or the Internet he's not interested. That's so stupid! Mom said it was a big reason she had to go, and now he's worse than ever. You try to talk to him and you can tell he just wants to get back to programming."

"Geez, Sandy, I'm sorry," Jeremy said. He thought about holding her hand to make her feel better, but he wasn't sure she'd like it.

"Well, there's nothing you can do about it, anyways," Sandy snapped, kicking hard at a pinecone on the sidewalk.

Jeremy had the feeling that if he *had* touched her she might have kicked *him* instead. "What did Zack say about the TV?" he asked, booting the pinecone farther along.

"A bunch of stuff about electrons and polarity," Sandy answered, making a face as she took another kick. "He was just showing off, as usual."

13

3 SERIOUS WEIRDNESS

When Jeremy got home, around one o'clock, his dad was in the recliner working on a crossword puzzle and his mom was setting the dining room table. They both looked tired. Mom was moving slowly, as if under water, but she found enough energy to give Jeremy a quick smile.

"There's still some sliced ham in the fridge." she told him. "If you're hungry, I can make you a sandwich."

"Thanks, Mom," Jeremy replied, "but you look busy. I'll do it." He slapped some meat between two slices of whole-wheat bread and poured himself a glass of milk at the counter. Sara sat in the breakfast nook, staring at the wall.

"Hey Sar," Jeremy asked, already munching on his sandwich, "do you want some?" It was as if she hadn't heard him—no, worse, she made him feel as if he'd never even asked. And that really bugged him, so he answered for her. "Hello, Jeremy. Glad to see you. But no thanks, I'm not really hungry."

"Jeremy," his mother said coolly, "teasing her won't help."

"Geez, Mom," Jeremy began, and then paused while he gulped his milk. "I wasn't teasing her. I was just trying to get her to say *something*." He wiped his mouth on his sleeve and turned away before they really started arguing. She said nothing more, and he imagined her face relaxing a bit as she decided to let it go.

Cleopatra, Jeremy's cat, padded in and sat down in the doorway. She curled her tail neatly around herself and examined everyone with great interest. Suddenly, Sara turned her head and looked straight at Cleo. "Red wigglers," Sara

14

whispered, as she had done, now and then, for a few days— "red wigglers all over."

Cleo padded up to Sara and peered into her eyes, her ears twitching as if Sara were still speaking. Jeremy's dad glanced up from his puzzle and met his mother's gaze. They sighed and sat perfectly still, each in a little shadow of sadness.

What Sara had said brought to Jeremy's mind the image of the red wiggling creature in the pond water, but he pushed it away. It had to be a coincidence. Bored with all the heavy stuff and wanting nothing more than to play, he dragged a catnip-filled rubber mouse in front of Cleo.

Jeremy twitched the toy in what he thought was a very mouse-like way, but Cleo evidently didn't think so. She sniffed it, poked it once with her paw, and walked away. Then she sat down like a queen on her throne, wrapped herself in her tail, and peered intently at a dark corner of the living room.

A small, long-haired black cat, Cleo could walk into a shadow and disappear. Now she did just that, stalking down the hallway toward Jeremy's bedroom with ears perked and whiskers twitching. She stared piercingly at nothing Jeremy could see, but he suspected Cleo saw far more than he could.

He sighed and flopped belly-down on the living room rug, chin propped on his folded arms. The rug was a Persian carpet his father had bought while he was a doctor in the Navy, taking care of Marines, long before Jeremy was born. "Is it a flying carpet, Dad?" Jeremy remembered asking when he was little.

"If you know the magic words," his father had answered, "but they're in Persian."

"Well, what are they?"

"They're secret, but I'll whisper them in your ear. 'Wash-up-and-get-ready-for-dinner!'"

"That's not Persian," Jeremy had yelled, squealing and rolling around on the rug as his dad tickled his ribs. Dad had always been like that, playing tricks and fooling around. Until lately.

Jeremy would have played video games, but he'd run the ones he had a hundred times. So he went on thinking about what life was like before the trouble started. A castle surrounded by purple and red flowers was woven into the center of the carpet. When he was a lot younger, he'd played marbles there, flicking his thumb to send a red warrior crashing into a platoon of greens protecting villagers in the castle. The green warriors blocked the red one and the people were saved.

Jeremy had imagined the castle was an ancient stronghold defended by a few brave knights against barbarian hordes or an attacking dragon. Then it became an alien space prison for hostages that astronauts had to rescue, or a jungle city attacked by giant mutant gorillas.

He smiled at the memory of passing whole afternoons on the rug. No way would he play those kid games now, though it would be really neat if he were a programmer and could develop them into video games. But he wasn't, and now the castle was just a boring old picture on a boring old carpet.

In the kitchen, Mom and Dad hunched over their coffee and talked quietly. Jeremy couldn't hear what they were saying, but they frowned and looked worried. It had to be the same conversation as always lately, what to do about Sara. To avoid thinking about that, Jeremy went back to remembering.

His dad had played tennis on a team in college, and he'd been teaching Jeremy the game every weekend. It was really cool and Jeremy was getting pretty good. Mentally, he replayed some of his best shots, but then realized that they had not played for a whole month and started thinking about Sara again, just as his parents were.

He was twelve and Sara was just eight, but they still spent time together and played with each other. She had been his live-wire little sister, and now she was sick—a special kind of sickness, Mom had explained, that the doctors couldn't figure out. The week after Grandpa had died, late one stormy night, Sara had started doing seriously weird things.

Jeremy remembered it now as clearly as if it were all happening again. A few days after the funeral, on a Sunday afternoon, his mom had taken him by the arm, her face screwed tight with worry. "Jerry," she'd said anxiously, "have you seen Sara? We've been looking all afternoon and she's simply disappeared."

When Jeremy found her, Sara was at the corner gas station, staring into the pit beneath the metal tracks that held up cars while the mechanics worked under them. Somehow, she'd slipped past the garage men.

"Sar!" he yelled, "what are you doing in there? Mom and Dad are real worried." She looked at him as if she didn't know who he was.

Then Sara turned her head slowly and asked, in a puzzled voice, "Is Grandpa in *this* hole? When will he come out?"

Jeremy's parents explained which hole Grandpa *was* in, and why, but it didn't help. She needed more than to cherish Gramps in her memory, and she went on disappearing. Frantic, they would find her quietly studying some hole: the one at the gas station, a drainage ditch in the field down the block, or the one for the foundation of the new supermarket.

At home, Sara would stare at nothing, whisper nonsense to herself, and sometimes behave like a crazy baby, screaming and giggling, shouting swear words. A week ago, she'd picked up her plate of spaghetti, dumped it on the floor, and started twirling around in the middle of the mess while the whole family watched with their mouths hanging open. When Mom tried to stop her, Sara had flailed at her with both fists as hard as she could.

Jeremy cringed to remember his sweet sister behaving like a raving maniac. Could all this really be just because she missed Gramps?

He moved from the Persian rug to the space behind the couch along the living room wall. This was one of his favorite spots—hidden and quiet, where he was like a spy who could hear anything anybody said in the house. The bare floor was hard and cool against his back, and had the comforting scent of the orange wood cleaner his mom used.

Jeremy ran his fingers around the squares of the grate that covered the floor vent, playing tic-tac-toe on them without really thinking about it, and watched the dust float in the sunlight streaming through the picture window. His mother's voice reached him from the kitchen, soft but angry.

"Farber thinks there's something wrong with Sara's brain," she said to his father. "Well I can't accept that. She's just very upset because Dad died. Hell, I'm still upset and it's been two months! My father filled Sara's head with Egyptian myths about life after death. The same stories he told me. But I didn't have Sara's imagination, and he didn't go and die on me. She's just missing him terribly, Ben, and waiting for him to come back. She'll get better."

"I don't know what to say, Laurie," Jeremy's father sighed. "Maybe she loved Heinrich too much. He was an impressive guy, but you have to admit he was pretty full of himself, and he had both the kids almost worshipping him. I think maybe he loved that more than them. Remember, I told you we should get him to tone that down—but we never did have that talk. So maybe Sara just misses him, but Farber's a respected psychiatrist, and if he says there's more to it . . ."

"Oh, you doctors always stick together," Jeremy's mom interrupted sharply. "You'd rather accept what some stranger says than your own wife's common sense. Don't you think I've been a teacher and a mother long enough to know something about kids?"

Then came silence, except for the rustle of the weekend newspaper as his father turned a page. It was far from the first time Jeremy had overheard this conversation, or something similar. He studied a bar of afternoon sunlight connecting the window to the far wall, and imagined himself so small and light that he could walk up it like a path and lose himself in the pure blue sky.

That morning, as he'd stood in front of the bathroom mirror, a skinny boy with thick brown hair and a few freckles on his flat cheeks had looked back. A boy with a narrow forehead, a small, straight nose, and a dimpled chin. That was Jeremy, and nobody else. He ran his tongue over the rough chip in one of his top front teeth, where an ice-ball thrown by a rotten older kid had hit him two winters ago. He studied his own green eyes as they stared back at him from the mirror. Maybe I could see clear through to my brain, he thought, concentrating as hard as he could.

It didn't work, of course. The glass wasn't deep enough, or his vision wasn't strong enough. But what if he could turn his eyes all the way around and look back into his head, see his brain all coiled and gray like the one his teacher had in a jar? What if his brain was hurt, like Sara's? "Red wigglers," he'd tried whispering to himself, half expecting to see one swimming across the mirror. But nothing changed. Jeremy stared into the glass and Jeremy stared back.

Had he done anything to harm Sara? Sometimes he teased her, a devilish urge he couldn't resist, but usually she'd laugh or tease him back. Sometimes he'd get too rough or go on too long and she'd start crying, but that couldn't hurt her, could it? If Grandpa Heinrich were still alive, he could help her, Jeremy thought, though no one else seemed able to.

He remembered playing in his grandfather's apartment in the city, just a few months ago. Grandpa seemed fine, though he was over seventy. He was still teaching ancient history at the college, and his place was so stuffed with old books that there was hardly room for anything else. Jeremy liked everything about the musty old apartment, full of antique things from Grandpa's travels in the East and the spicy smell of pipe smoke.

More than anything, he loved reading with his grandfather, bending at his side over thick, leather-bound books, tickled by his broad, bushy beard. Together, they looked at pictures and absorbed stories of long-forgotten times, imagining in rich detail whatever the books left out. They studied maps of the ancient world and its nations, following the routes of camel caravans and forgotten armies. Even the names of the old peoples were magical: Persians, Amelekites, Philistines, Hittites, Assyrians, Egyptians.

Grandpa Heinrich had promised to take Jeremy to Egypt when he got older, to see the great Pyramids and the Sphinx. Meanwhile, they spent many afternoons in the Museum of Natural History, marveling at the tomb of the mummy and learning about Egyptian myths and religion. But now Grandpa was gone, like all the ancient kings and queens.

Jeremy lay still behind the couch as silence took over the house. Though sunlight poured in through the window, he felt cold. He wanted someone to find him and talk to him, but nobody did. He lay quiet, feeling grayer and lonelier every second, until Cleopatra streaked around the corner and jumped onto his chest, purring like a drum roll.

She dug her claws through his tee shirt, not enough to hurt but as if she were gently kneading dough, and looked greedily into his eyes. He stroked her soft black fur slowly, the way she liked, passing both hands from the tip of her nose down to the end of her tail.

Cleo crept right up to Jeremy's face, kneading deliriously, twitching her tail in delight. Her green-gold eyes shone into his as she licked drying tears from his cheek with her raspy tongue.

Jeremy thought how much he loved Cleo, and how alone he would be if anything happened to her. Then he felt, creeping up in him, the same delicious urge to tease her that he felt with Sara. He knew Cleo didn't like being suspended above the ground, but he slid his hands inside her forelegs, where her armpits would be if she were human, swung her up into the air, and dangled her at arm's length.

Cleo hung there for a moment, perfectly still, as if she wanted to give him a chance to behave himself and bring her back down. But he decided to hold her up just a little longer and move his arms back and forth as if she were on a swing.

As though she read his mind, Cleo's eyes flashed a warning and she wriggled loose, gave a low yowl, and was gone, her tail batting his cheek as she sailed around the couch. He was sad to lose her, but couldn't help feeling gleeful about ruffling her usual calm. He could be a really rotten kid sometimes—he knew it, but something got into him and he just couldn't help it.

"Jeremy," his mother's voice called, "What have you been doing to that cat? She just flew past here like lightning."

"Aw Mom, I didn't do anything. She must have felt like running. Just because something happens doesn't mean I did it."

"Why are you still inside, Jerry," his father added. "If you won't go out, at least practice your violin. We paid good money for that instrument."

Jeremy propped himself on his elbow. "Dad!" he nearly yelled with exasperation, "I practiced my dumb violin yesterday, didn't you hear me? And I don't want to go outside—why bother when there's almost nobody to play with in this stupid neighborhood. You took Sara over to Aunt Lillian's, remember?"

Jeremy's mother appeared in the living room, hands on hips, frowning down at him as he sprawled on the floor. "Don't make excuses to your father, Jerry," she said in a tight voice. "You need to play with kids your own age, not just Sara. Why don't you go see Zack and Sandy?"

"I was just there," Jeremy complained as he got up, "and Sandy and I got into a fight with Zack. You only want me out of here so you can talk about Sara all day. Geez, Mom, why did Gramps have to go and die, anyway?"

His mother's voice turned shrill. "Come here, Jeremy," she snapped, retreating to the den. Jeremy hung back as she sat down, dreading the lecture that was coming. "You get in here this instant!" she commanded. Sighing, he trudged into the den, slouched against the wall, and stared at the floor.

"Come right over here and look at me," she said, pointing at an empty chair until Jeremy sat down. But then she took his face in her hands and her voice softened. Jeremy felt like Cleo must have as he'd dangled her above him at arm's length.

"Everybody's upset now, Jeremy. It's not your grandfather's fault and it's not yours either—it's just a bad time. But it will be over soon, Sara will get better, and we'll have fun again. You'll see. Now go outside and play."

"Mom," Jeremy said, "Grandpa never meant for Sara to believe those stories. All that stuff about the mummy coming back to life and killing those guys who disturbed his tomb. It was like fun ghost stories around a campfire. And he really did love *us*, not just us loving *him*."

"Jeremy," his father said sternly, walking into the den, "have you been snooping?"

"Never mind, Ben," his mother answered. "It's all right. I know Grandpa didn't mean to cause Sara pain," she said to Jeremy, "but she has a very strong imagination and she's too young to think things through. She believes anything you tell her. Now, go outside and play before you upset your father again. You know how easy that is!"

She forced a grin at her husband, hiding her sadness behind kidding, but Jeremy saw through it. She caught his arm as he turned away and gave him a quick hug and a kiss on the forehead. "We love you, Jerry," she said.

"Yes," his father added, managing to make a funny face at his wife and then rumpling Jeremy's thick brown hair. "We love you, Jeremy. And we'll have more tennis lessons soon."

"I love you too," Jeremy said, thinking of his dad's strong hands moving his own skinny arms into position for each shot, his dad who never chewed him out when he screwed up,

22

which was a lot, as long as he tried his best. "I just wish things could be normal again."

Jeremy turned and slouched out of the kitchen, dragging his feet so his sneakers squeaked on the linoleum. "But I don't think Sara's going to get better," he muttered, almost out of earshot. "You're just telling me that so *I'll* feel better."

"Jeremy!" his mother gasped, "how dare you say that! Get back here, now!" But Jeremy, already out the back door and halfway down the steps, felt as relieved to get away as Cleo must have after she'd escaped his grasp. He didn't turn around.

4 THE GOLDEN SPIDER

Jeremy broke into a run as soon as he left his yard and kept on running, to no particular place, until he finally ran out of breath. It was such a relief just to be moving, going somewhere even if it was nowhere, and not stuck in the mud of his problems. He walked for a while, kicking a stone, until he noticed that he wasn't seeing sunlight on the sidewalk any more, and looked up.

The distant clouds that had started gathering earlier now spread across the sky, and a peal of thunder turned him toward home and shelter at a fast walk. Just as the rain started he jogged up the front walk and snuck quickly into his room to avoid talking to anyone. Then he sat on his bed watching raindrops spatter the window and race each other down to the sill. Within twenty minutes, sunshine found its way back through the departing clouds and the quick storm was over.

Jeremy opened the window and lay on his bed, arms behind his head, feeling the still clammy air and listening to the occasional hiss of car tires on the wet road. The ceiling, freshly painted white when they'd moved into this new suburban house, was like a snow-covered plain, with no trails or tracks.

That was the future, he thought, the winter soon to come. Maybe Zack and he would continue exploring the area, as they had over the summer, by bike if the snow was plowed and on foot if not. If Zack and he were still speaking by then.

Their friendship had begun in early June when they had accidentally crashed together coasting up to the school bike rack. Zack fell to the ground, his bike across his legs, and Jeremy toppled elbows first onto his chest.

24

"Geez," Zack groaned through clenched teeth, "you're as heavy as *Bubalis carabanesis*, and you sank my floating rib."

"What?" Jeremy answered, bewildered. He got the bike off Zack and into the rack, helped him up, and sat down with him against a tree, where Zack explained that *B carabensis* was a "carabao," a type of Asian water buffalo, and a floating rib was a "detached ventral rib distal to the others."

"Okay," Jeremy replied, "now tell me in English."

"Smart-ass," Zack grinned, though the word described him better than Jeremy. Then Zack launched into such a lecture about anatomy that Jeremy thought he'd learned enough to graduate from high school. That day Zack taught him some new chess openings—he'd learned the game from his dad but never studied it much—and beat him in five straight games.

But when Zack saw that Jeremy was looking downhearted, he showed his student where he'd made mistakes and helped improve his game. They agreed to discover their new neighborhood together, "like Lewis and Clark," Zack had exclaimed, continuing Jeremy's education by describing the two great explorers' trip from St. Louis to the Pacific Ocean.

Zack was driven not only to learn everything, Jeremy realized as he got to know him, but also to teach it to everyone else. "Hey, check this out," he'd begin with a goofy grin, and then go on to explain some bit of knowledge that excited him, not so much to show off as to help you understand as much as he did, so you could appreciate it together.

Zack's smile of eager delight as he explained the world, and his goofy intensity, were more excitement about having somebody to talk to and teach than trying to mock or insult anyone—or at least that's what Jeremy had thought until that morning. Now he wasn't so sure.

The new ceiling waited, as he did, for something to happen, to leave a mark on its blankness. A breeze through the window licked Jeremy's bare wrist. His thumb rubbed the smooth surface of the black stone Grandpa Heinrich had brought him from Egypt. It was a small, flat rectangle with

25

rounded corners, and on it was carved a raised ankh, the ancient Egyptian symbol for life. Jeremy's thumb traced the carving, following the loop and then the cross at its base.

The Ankh

The stone was gleaming black obsidian. It had a hole for a thong in one end, but Jeremy's mother wouldn't let him wear it around his neck because she was afraid he'd lose it or get it caught in something and damage it—or himself. "It's special," she said, "so you should keep it somewhere safe and special."

But Grandpa had said the ankh would bring good luck to the bearer, even better than a rabbit's foot. So Jeremy carried it in his pants pocket every day, but was careful to put it in his cedarwood box of treasures at night so his mom wouldn't discover it in the pocket of his dirty pants when she did the wash. Now, as he rubbed his thumb over its smooth surface, it calmed him in spite of everything going on.

Why would his mother blame Grandpa Heinrich for Sara's illness and then say later on that it wasn't Gramps's fault? Things were so confusing. He'd listened to Gramps's stories along with Sara, but *he* didn't believe that dead people came back to life or that mummies walked or any of that stuff.

Like the myth about the evil god Seth tearing to pieces the good god Osiris, whose son Horus then fought Seth down through the ages. At last Horus won and Osiris's wife Isis dug up his parts and put him together again. Horus, the Hawk, the Avenger. Seth, the Destroyer. It was a neat story, but nobody believed it. Except for Sara.

What if it's really my fault, not Gramps's, Jeremy thought. Had he been too rough on Sara when he was tickling her or play-wrestling, as Mom thought? Did he hurt Sara without meaning to? Or did he mean it, just a little? Maybe he was tired of being told to take care of his little sister, and how much his parents worried about her. Maybe he was really just a nasty kid. As he thought this, shame and sadness surrounded him like a broad, heavy shadow, a dark lake from which some monstrous thing rose, gazed directly at him, and then slowly sank back into the depths.

Jeremy sighed and gently shook his head, remembering something and trying not to at the same time. One incredibly boring Sunday afternoon, he'd gotten Sara to play catch with him in the back yard. He tossed the football to her underhand, careful to keep it slow, until she stopped and shouted, "Come on, Jer, throw it for real!"

"That would be too hard for you, Sar," he'd replied, "you might get hurt."

"No I won't," Sara said, pouting, "I can catch it. I'm a big girl. Mom says so."

"Okay, Sar, run eight steps down, turn right, run three more steps, and then turn and look at me."

Jeremy took her hike, waited until she ran down and two steps out, and then zinged the ball toward her far harder than he'd intended to. And she was so into running that she forgot to turn. The ball hit the side of her head and, falling, she bashed her head again on the turf. Why did I throw so hard? Jeremy asked himself now, for the hundredth time.

He was proud of his strong arm, that could be it. Or maybe it was like when he was being too rough or teasing her too much—he got this evil urge and couldn't resist. He thought of Sara lying on the ground, stunned, crying. He hadn't wanted to hurt her, had he? He'd gone over and gently hugged her and talked to her till she stopped crying, and then wiped her face with his shirt. She promised not to tell because then he'd be in real trouble, and she didn't want that. But not long after he'd beaned her, she started getting weird.

If it was his fault, he wished he could make up for it, and even if it wasn't, he wished he could help somehow. But he couldn't even talk about it. The worst had been when his mom had asked him if he knew whether something had happened to Sara, something that might have upset her. "After all, Jerry," she'd continued with an encouraging smile, "you spend more time with her than we do."

Jeremy had felt like he'd been stabbed in the chest with a large, sharp icicle, and his heart, jumping like a tortured frog, had leapt into his throat to avoid it. "Jeremy," his mom probed, puzzled by his panicked look, "is there anything you need to tell me?"

"No Mom," he'd choked out, "I'm just really worried about Sar, that's all." This was the pits—having to lie to his own mother because he was too cowardly to admit what he might have done and face the consequences. He couldn't take the risk of knowing for sure that he had messed up Sara and having them hate him for the rest of his life—even though they might actually have told him that he hadn't harmed her at all. Jeremy just couldn't take the risk. Instead, with all of his heart he wished there were some way, some idea he could try, to fix Sara and make his terrible secret irrelevant, just as an antivenin cured the poison of a snake bite.

But what could he do? He was just a regular kid, not a genius or a miracle worker. His grades were okay but not great, and he really sucked in math—C's most of the time. If only he got all A's like Zack, or was a nicer, braver person, like Sandy, maybe he could figure out something. Jeremy blew his breath out through his mouth and vibrated his lips, making the disgusted, snorting sound of an irritated horse.

"Don't just lie around and feel sorry for yourself, Jeremy," he imagined his mom's voice lecturing him. "Go out and do something!" But he didn't want to do something. He didn't want to do anything.

"I'm not just feeling sorry for myself," he answered. "Things really are crappy and I'm not helping any." He made another snorting noise, opened his eyes, and resumed staring at the ceiling. From the corner of his eye, he saw the clock on his bedside table showing three-fifteen.

A low rumble of thunder sounded in the distance. From far away came the thin, sad whistle of a passing train. Jeremy wondered what sort of people were on the train, and where they were going. You couldn't get to Egypt on a train. But what if he could just beam himself there with a transporter? He'd join up with a famous Egyptologist, and together they'd ride camels out into the desert and find lost tombs and ancient cities. He'd be like Indiana Jones, fighting cut-throat thieves trying to steal magic stuff and use it for evil. He'd burst over the tops of dunes riding an Arabian stallion, cut down hordes of reborn mummies with his scimitar, rescue Sandy—she could come too—from the pit of poisonous snakes where the marauders threw her, and she would . . .

Nah, he whispered gloomily, cutting short his daydream. In reality, with Gramps gone, he'd never get to Egypt. He was stuck in his house, and he wouldn't be going anywhere. Nothing ever happens, he thought as he got sleepier. It feels like something will, like it should, but it never does.

A spider dropped from the ceiling to within a few feet of Jeremy's nose. A big, scary spider on a strand, swaying gently in the breeze from the window, probably getting ready to jump on him and bite. Jeremy hated spiders. They frightened him, like so many things. Now his stomach convulsed in disgust as, watching the creature from the corner of his eye, he rolled over and reached toward the floor for his sneaker. Even if he was too chicken to fight, he had enough guts to deal with a spider.

He grabbed the sneaker and rolled to a sitting position, ready to whack the arachnid—a scientific word for spider that Zack had taught him—but something stopped him. He paused and looked more closely in the late afternoon sunlight filtering through his window. It wasn't a black, a brown, or even a gray spider. It was golden, glinting on a shining silver strand, and it held perfectly still, as if watching him as he watched it. Without knowing why, he relaxed and let himself fall back on his pillow.

The spider rubbed a front leg slowly across its strand, like a bow across a stringed instrument. Jeremy couldn't believe his eyes or his ears, for the bow made high, sweet music, like a violin. He stuck his fingers in his earholes, but the melody continued. With a quick shudder, he realized that he was hearing it not with his ears, but in his mind. It was a song and there were words and Jeremy understood them.

> I come for a Guardian
> To see us safe home
> I come for a hero
> To make himself known.

The spider dropped toward Jeremy's face. He saw tiny hairs on its body glisten as it passed through bars of sunlight from the window. Then he saw what could not be. The spider had twelve legs. Jeremy blinked, but there it was. He knew he should be afraid, but actually he wasn't. I must be dreaming, he thought, but his eyes were wide open.

The spider played again, and its song seemed to come all at once from near and far away. "Alaikin am I, from beyond the sky. To you I come, for you are the one." The musical words bathed Jeremy's skin like moonbeams and webbed his mind like silvery cotton candy—so cool and sweet it ached—and then went on.

Jeremy is chosen
Keeper of the peace,
Jeremy the brave,
Tamer of the Beast.

If Jeremy comes,
The stars will rise.
If Jeremy stays,
The Dragon flies.

"Watch, Jeremy."

The spider pointed its legs at the twelve hours of the clock. From the tip of each leg, a silver thread stretched like a spoke, straight out, parallel to the floor, as if gravity didn't exist. Circular strands branched off, connecting the spokes in a web wheel that grew out and out until it was as wide as Jeremy was tall. When the finished wheel hovered shimmering above, the spider's words formed in Jeremy's mind, to music as clear and silvery as ice melting on a moonlit night.

"Do not be frightened, Earth-child. The way is hard and the dangers many, but you have been chosen. You shall call me Alaikin—for on my planet, and in the starry reach beyond, that is my name—and I shall help you on your journey. Watch now, Jeremy, and I will show."

The web wheel began to spin. Jeremy squeezed his eyes shut until they hurt, but he still saw the web spinning, slowly at first and then picking up speed. "Now I know this is a dream," he murmured, "or I couldn't see it. So whatever happens, it won't matter anyway."

"Whether you wake or whether you dream," Alaikin replied, "you must see what must be seen."

First I will show.
Then you will know:
Come or stay,

Choose what you may,
We will obey.

Jeremy opened his eyes again. The web spun still faster, and the music drifted through his mind like incense. At last, hanging in midair, a great silvery mirror faced him. He saw a small boy lying in bed, fists clenched and eyes wide. Then a hot wind rushed from the mirror, smelling of burning pine.

Jeremy saw his reflection ripple and disappear. Flames whirled through a forest and animals ran before the red, rolling wave. A fox leapt across the mirror and stared out, its terrified eyes glinting in the firelight. Rabbits scattered everywhere and deer sprang wildly, as if lifted by the heated air.

"What is it?" Jeremy whispered. "What does it mean?"

"Watch!" commanded Alaikin.

Smoke boiled from the fire and billowed across the mirror. When it cleared, everything had changed. A burnt city smoldered and hundreds of weeping people wandered, searching among the cinders, their tears gray with ash.

Jeremy's own eyes were wet. "Spider—I mean Alaikin," he asked, amazed to be speaking to the creature as if it were real, "What happened? What are they looking for?"

"They seek what they have lost, and when they find it, they will lose it again. Watch," commanded Alaikin. "Now is for watching; later, for telling."

A gray mist filled the mirror and covered the desolate city. When it melted away, Jeremy gazed into a night sky filled with flame-blue stars. Like a giant, glittering carousel, the sky slowly spun. Clusters of stars swung past like ripe blue fruit in an immense wind. At last, one star loomed so close that Jeremy saw its planets, gravely circling in the silver-blue light. Alaikin's music haunted his mind once more as a friendly planet parted its clouds. Jeremy looked down on a green meadow bursting with flowers.

Two creatures of human size and shape, but covered with downy fur the color of honey, played together in the grass.

One picked an armful of flowers and flung it over the other, and then they laughed and rolled in the sweet-smelling meadow. Jeremy sensed their love, so strong it flowed out to him. He wanted to bury his face in their fur and tumble in their gentle play, but he could only watch. Their large, golden eyes were mild and wondering, and they spread their arms in welcome. But the mist closed in again, and they were gone.

Space and stars wheeled past, and by now Jeremy had forgotten his room, forgotten himself lying on his bed. Like a small, bright fish in a deep lake, he swam through the night of the galaxy. Suddenly, a dark star loomed close, its shine tarnished to dull gray. The dreary light of this dim sun barely touched one lone, dismal planet, a bleak and icy world. Alaikin's melody sank beneath a spiteful, shrieking noise, as if a monstrous steel beam were twisting and snapping.

Jeremy tried to turn away but was dragged helplessly down to the planet. On gritty soil scorched like crumbling lava, he stood facing an enormous cave a half-mile wide and two football fields high. The mouth of the cave was dark. The acrid odor of ammonia reached out for him. From deep within came a low, booming sound, huge and slow, like giant waves pounding on a beach.

Jeremy could not turn away. He was pushed closer and closer, as if by a powerful wind. Lightning forked the cave's dark throat and the fierce ammonia odor stabbed his nose and eyes. Suddenly, white terror flashed through him as he recognized the sound that boomed in black waves. It was the sure, ferocious beating of an enormous heart.

His mouth opened to scream—opened so wide he thought his head would turn inside-out—but the sound was sucked away before it passed his lips. From deep in the cave came vast, hollow laughter, harsh and mocking, so fully evil that his bones seemed to twist in his flesh to escape the sound. Then everything disappeared, and he was asleep.

5 READY, SET . . .

Jeremy awoke to a cool evening breeze that ruffled the curtains and nuzzled his bare shoulder. His throat was dry and his eyes burned as if someone had set off a flash bulb in his face. His hand ached, and when he opened it, there was the ankh stone. He had gripped it hard enough to bruise his palm.

For a moment, Jeremy's mind was blank, drained of all memory. But when he closed his eyes again, the dream seeped back: the golden spider and the mirror of Space, the fire and the ruined city, the gentle creatures of the friendly planet, and then—the nightmare.

Re-living the shock of that desolate planet, Jeremy shuddered. It had seemed so real, but how could it be? Was he losing his mind, like Sara? Now the sweet, soothing melody of the golden spider trickled through his mind again. He opened his eyes slowly, praying that he would see nothing. What he did see was his door opening a crack and his mom peering in.

"Dinner," Jeremy, she said softly, "It's six o'clock—wash your hands and come to the table."

"Okay, Mom, I'll be right there," he answered, bathed in warm relief to see her softly smiling face and no spider, golden or otherwise.

Dinner was something his dad loved but he could just barely eat—liver and onions—but he was so happy to be home and not caught in a nightmare that he only wrinkled his nose and didn't complain. Maybe because he really liked dinner, his dad cheered up and started telling stories about his time in the Navy, and his mom fussed a bit about Jeremy's taking an afternoon nap at an age when he should be full of energy.

"You're not coming down with something, are you," she asked anxiously.

"He's fine, Laurie," his dad said firmly, in his best doctor's voice, "good complexion, good appetite—come on, he's even eating liver!" Then everybody except Sara started laughing. After dinner they watched a TV special about pro tennis, his dad explaining some of the game's finer points.

Jeremy started back to his room after the program, thinking he'd play some games. He grabbed his laptop, swung the door shut, spun, and flung himself across the room and onto his bed all in one motion.

"All right," he cheered to himself, thinking Sandy would be impressed, "Jeremy Taylor grabs the pass, hurdles a defender, and lands flat on his back but hangs onto that ball—touchdown!" From the corner of his eye, he caught a small motion near the window, and turned his head to see better.

Red-gold in the light of the setting sun, in a small web at the end of a strand, Alaikin swung gently in the breeze. Jeremy flung his arm over his face and closed his eyes tight. But he still saw it, as plain as if he were staring wide-eyed. "I can't believe this is happening," he moaned. "Why can't you be a dream? Go away and never come back!"

Alaikin's twelve legs moved gently over the silken web, and cool, silvery music welled again in Jeremy's mind, pushing his eyes open. "Do not fight me, child of Earth," sang the sweet voice. "The choice is yours. I will go if you wish. But you must not deny what you have seen."

"You showed me terrible things," Jeremy whispered. "How could I ever trust you?"

"Terrible things, Earth-child, but beautiful things, too, for such is the nature of your world, and the million million worlds beyond. Beauty and life, always, fear and death, forever. But, know that death is double in the universe."

35

"I'm not hearing this," Jeremy said, plugging his ears with his fingers. "You're not real and I don't know what you're talking about."

"Of course I am, and of course you don't," came the song, as clear and patient as before, "because you haven't let me explain. You know one kind of death, the kind that seems frightening but is actually beautiful—for all living beings are born from it, and to it they return. From this death, you came; to it, your grandfather returned, as you will, someday."

"How do you know about my Gramps?" Jeremy blurted, pulling his fingers out of his ears since they hadn't stopped Alaikin's voice for one second.

"A better question might be how did your grandfather know about me, Earth-one. Yet know me he did, and he served me well."

"How could Grandpa serve you?" Jeremy nearly yelled. "He never even met you. He told me all kinds of stuff and he never said a word about you!"

"The Guardians of Earth—*Ouyperkain Orthein* in the Primal Tongue—do not tell of their trust, Earth-child. They do their work in silence. I have sung to you of the Lesser Death, which is fertile, and like a mother gives birth to all life. This death balances with life on a seesaw that is the engine of the universe. But there is a Greater Death, a frozen terror beyond all time. It is sterile and brings forth nothing. It is absolute annihilation. And only the *Ouyperkain* stand against it."

"Okay," Jeremy snapped. "So you're saying Grandpa was one of these Guardians and there's all kinds of trouble because he died?"

"Now is a time when the Greater Death grows dense and heavy, a Time of Unbalance, when the seesaw swings wildly on its axis. If it falls off, the universe will fall, and all that is fine and alive will be destroyed. You and your fellow Guardians are chosen to help set the Balance right, to level the tilting seesaw."

36

"Why me?" Jeremy wailed. "Why pick on a little kid? You could get the President or somebody important!"

"I am the bearer of messages and answers," Alaikin sang, "and you are kin to a Guardian. Through my web I felt the tug of your name and the music of courage and kindness in your soul. And so, I came."

"Great," Jeremy muttered. "And what if I don't want to be 'chosen'? What if I don't want to be anything! I don't have any courage. I didn't even have the guts to fight Timmy Randall and his stupid brother—I tried to talk my way out of it, and when I couldn't, I ran away."

Jeremy felt his face flush with shame at the memory of losing his pocket knife to a pair of bullies the summer after fifth grade. His mom had to go to their mother in order to get it back. That couldn't be courage by anybody's definition, even a golden spider's.

"I'm not going to do it!" Jeremy shouted at the creature. "To hell with righting your Balance—it's a stupid idea anyway."

Alaikin didn't react to his outburst, but the Arkanian's twelve legs began rhythmically kneading the silver threads on which they rested. The web emitted low, vibrating sounds, like the strumming a distant train makes if you put your ear to the rail.

"What are you doing," Jeremy asked doubtfully.

"I seek another willing to become *Ouyperkai Orthein*. You have refused, and time is too short to debate with you."

Jeremy felt a lance of envy stab him in the guts, as if he'd been stung by a huge wasp. "Well, can't you wait a minute while I think about it? I mean, it's a lot to decide."

The low strumming continued and the web shivered with its rhythm. Alaikin made no other response.

"Spider," Jeremy said in a quavering voice, "Alaikin, come on. Give me a chance."

"You had your chance, Jeremy, and you refused it. Clearly, you are more concerned about yourself and your own special fears than about those you love. To think of your friends, Zack and Sandy, of your mother and father, of your sister, and of all who will suffer under the Dragon's lash—that has not even occurred to you.

"No, I will find someone less in love with his own fear and more with his fellow beings. I sense a signal strong as yours and more mature. Goodbye, Jeremy—I must go to Asia where she lives."

"Wait!" Jeremy whispered desperately, feeling not cool relief at his escape but the lance of envy now hot and twisting below his ribs. How would he live with himself if he chickened out and left this task to someone else—especially a girl!

"This isn't fair! You didn't tell me everything that was at stake. Sara!" Jeremy whispered. "Is she *really*—and everybody else—are they in that much danger?"

"Every living creature is in peril," Alaikin replied. "The Dragon grows stronger by the hour. You saw its cave. You heard it laugh. What more do you need to know?"

"So that's why you showed me that horrible planet. The Dragon—it's the Greater Death?"

"Yes—the Dragon embodies the Greater Death: it is the material form of the Death that returns no life. I showed you that cave so you would begin to know what words could never tell. You saw the destruction to come if the Dragon is not opposed. You witnessed the golden creatures who will vanish, and the beauty of the stars that will rot and fall.

"Now you know enough to choose, and choose you must. Do not let fear govern you, Jeremy. Believe in your courage, for you do have it. Now, time is crucial. You must say, 'stay' or 'come.'"

Alaikin hung motionless with limbs folded, a golden patience on a silver string. Jeremy's heart thudded against his ribs. It felt like the bullfrog he and his father had once caught, jumping and jumping against the net. Now he was sure that this was no dream—unbelievable, yes—but all too real.

The door to Jeremy's room nudged open and a black streak rushed through and soared onto the bed. Cleo sat tensely, swishing her tail and staring at the alien, now wisely retreating up its strand.

Cleo liked spiders: they were her favorite dessert after a main course of mouse. Jeremy had watched her crunch up big juicy ones in the house and garden, and sometimes he found them for her. Now, he reached out to grab his cat—but then stopped and drew back his hands. He watched Cleo's eyes fix on Alaikin, bright, tasty, hanging like a tempting fruit from a branch.

After all, he thought, even if this thing isn't *really* a spider, it's close enough to be pretty revolting. And if Cleo eats it, well—so much for having to choose anything. A hateful grin spread across his face and vicious laughter bubbled up within him. Cleo crouched and flattened her ears. Jeremy watched, in a trance, and the black laughter was acid in his throat.

Something was wrong, very wrong, and as Cleo tensed to spring, Jeremy realized what. The laughter inside him wasn't his. He'd heard it before—in the vast cave. He lunged for Cleo faster than he'd ever moved, and caught her in midair. Alaikin hung serenely above the bed. The Dragon's laughter faded. All was quiet in the darkening room, except for Jeremy's quick breathing.

Alaikin's song began again, a thin silver stream like its strand. "So, Earth-child, you have chosen!"

"Well, I wouldn't say that," Jeremy quickly replied. "But how did the Dragon get inside of me?"

"*Ordúrrg-Zaikh*, the Dragon's name in the Primal Tongue, means 'Everywhere-Everyone,' for it permeates all Space for all time and can find a place in any being. It feeds on the seeds of greed, fear, and hate planted in us all. If we recognize and reject it, then it must leave. But many do not know it, and the worst and weakest welcome it. Then hatred grows, feeding on its host like a worm on the pulp of an apple, leaving a hollow, bitter shell."

"I've never moved so fast in my life!" Jeremy said.

"Once you chose, I helped you react. What mattered was that you knew and resisted *Ordúrrg-Zaikh* and that you wanted to stop the cat—not whether you could."

"No way will I learn to pronounce that Dragon's name," Jeremy thought.

"Ah," but you *will* need to learn the Primal Tongue, at least the names of anything and anyone important. For this language is as old as the planets: its words line the roots of the universe and share the force of life itself. Use it anywhere and you will not be misunderstood."

"I'll try," Jeremy thought in response, "but Spanish is hard enough! You know, once I figured out that it wasn't really *me* who wanted you crunched—that you're pretty much okay even if you look like, well, a bug—then I didn't want Cleo to eat you anymore. Hey, you're hearing my thoughts as if they're out loud!"

The silver strands of the alien's web tightened until they strummed, and its body seemed to swell ever so slightly. "A bug?" the shocked silvery voice sang in Jeremy's mind. "A bloody bug!" it continued in stinging, definitely British tones, sour and brassy as a trumpet.

"Why, you little Earth-snit! First you want to feed me to your cat, and then you call me the most disgraceful word in English. You may turn out to be Dragon-food after all, even if you *have* been chosen. And yes—I do *indeed* hear everything that goes on in your head, and anyone else's if I care to listen. Cleo's, for instance: I knew she had no intention of snacking on me. She was merely helping me help you to make up your bloody mind!"

Jeremy was so surprised that he said—or rather thought— nothing. Just when he'd almost gotten used to the spider it had changed completely. He looked down at Cleopatra, as if she could tell him what to do. She purred ecstatically in his arms, content as could be, as if nothing had changed. He stroked her, and she made a little gurgling noise and lifted her head. Her green-gold eyes, nearly the spider's color, shone steadily into his. She, too, seemed to be waiting for him to decide.

Jeremy looked at the alien again, dangling motionless on its strand. Alaikin had powers he couldn't imagine, and might tear him to bits if it got really mad. But so far, though he'd nearly let Cleo eat it and had insulted it, the creature seemed merely grumpy, not murderous.

Something told him to trust Alaikin. Somehow, he knew that nothing would ever be normal again unless he believed in the alien. His whole body began to prickle with excitement. Suddenly he was sure that there'd never really been a choice at all—he had decided long before Alaikin came. He took a huge breath and let it out.

"I'm sorry, Spider" he thought. "I'll never call you a—that b-word—again. And I will come with you, wherever we need to go."

"Sorry myself," answered Alaikin, as calmly as if Jeremy had merely agreed to go for a walk. "Actually, I'm grateful you gave me a chance to drop that stuffy cosmic speech I'm supposed to use at first meetings. It's terribly impressive, but what a bore! Now that we'll be traveling companions, would you mind if I keep the accent I picked up my last time on Earth, when I spent a few years in a lovely English garden?"

"That's okay, I guess," Jeremy thought doubtfully, "but you haven't even told me where we're going!"

"Oh, just for a quick jaunt across the universe. I'll explain it later: now we must get started. Cleo would like to come too—it seems the field mice have become too cautious, and she's rather bored."

"Okay," Jeremy said, a little scared but more excited. "Where's our ship?"

Tingling silvery laughter brushed through his mind. "Oh, Earth-sort, do you really think you need to get into some kind of spaceship? Quite the contrary—I will get into you, and you will be our 'ship.' I shall meld with both you and Cleo, for if I

41

were not inside you, you would explode in the nothingness of outer Space and be crushed by the everythingness of Time. The pressure of all that has ever happened or will happen would implode you to a nanopoint. Very messy, I assure you. Cleo will be first: you can watch her melding so you won't be afraid. But you don't fear me anymore, do you?"

"Umm, I guess not," Jeremy said nervously, scooting back a little on his bed as the spider glided down its silver strand. When it approached him, its body began to pulse slowly and then to spin, faster and faster, until it formed a glowing sphere haloed by golden light. The sphere split into two smaller beads, one of which zoomed into Cleo's left eye and disappeared. She purred in rapture as golden energy rippled through her, and Jeremy felt its warmth and brilliance lap over onto him. Alaikin's musical words welled in his mind.

"You first named me 'Spider,' Earth-child, and though inaccurate, that is at least respectful, for the spider has its place in the web of all that holds your Earth together. It is a name I could accept, in honor of all Earth-beings. But now you know my proper name, Alaikin, which in the Primal Tongue means 'One of Many.' Know also that I am really not an arachnid but one of myriad Arkanians, all sharing a single consciousness whatever our separate forms. Just as I—or rather we—are within Cleopatra, so we will now be within you."

The remaining gold bead dropped from the strand and zoomed into Jeremy's left eye faster than he could blink. The power of the Arkanian pulsed through his veins and lit his body with warm flame. He felt like a ripe peach, bursting with energy, clothed in a down of golden light. When his room, his house, and everyone he loved faded away, he wasn't afraid. Well, not much.

6 ANOTHER SPACE, ANOTHER TIME

Absolutely nothing existed beyond the thin cocoon of golden light that surrounded Jeremy. He saw nothing but the glow of the light, felt nothing but its warmth and Cleo's fur against his bare arms, and heard nothing but Alaikin's melody and Cleo's sleepy purr. As he basked in the golden glow, the Arkanian's words sang quietly in his mind.

"You and Cleo are now protected by my energy. It's what *you* might call a force field. I can create this field only in living cells, but it overlaps a bit beyond your skin, so it keeps you and your clothing inside and everything else outside. At this moment there is nothing at all outside, for we are in space beyond Space and time beyond Time. You Earth-ones would call this another dimension, but because we use this place to journey far, Arkanians call it by a special name. *Dimshen-cardác* in the Primal Tongue, in English it is 'Travel-on.' Are you quite comfortable, Jeremy?"

"This is super-weird!" Jeremy thought back. "It's as if I'm rolled up in a golden blanket, or a Christmas present wrapped in gold foil. When do I get opened?"

The Arkanian's music went staccato through a few low notes, a quick melodic chuckle. "You wouldn't want me to unwrap you here, Earth-child, for you'd become a very messy gift indeed. But the journey will not be long. Bypassing ordinary Space is the fastest way to get around the universe, though it means that we must also bypass ordinary Time. To re-enter Space, we will have to pass through everything that ever happened or ever will happen between our starting point and our destination. Actually, we will start from both ends of

43

Time at once, leaving the 'now' where we were and arriving in the 'now' where we will be."

"What?" Jeremy thought. "Maybe Zack would know what you're talking about, but I sure don't."

Alaikin's melody cascaded down a few octaves, a silvery glissando suspiciously like a musical giggle. "I'm sorry, Earth-child, but you truly are amusing. Let me try again. Suppose you took a trip in your parents' car and someone filmed everything along your route. Now, if you took the same trip outside Space and Time, you would never actually arrive unless that film was played back all at once from start to end and end to start. The catch is that you would be in the film too. Well, you'll see. We call it *Tyrdd-cayzh*—Time-crunch in English—and you will find it rather like viewing fireworks through a kaleidoscope."

"It sounds as if I'm going to be car-sick," Jeremy thought grumpily. "I hate when that happens. Can't you at least tell me where we're going? And when we'll get there?"

The music resumed its soothing, silvery tone, and Alaikin's voice cooed gently in Jeremy's mind. "Don't fret, Earth-one, we are almost there. It's not a long trip really, only to the center of the universe. That is where you are wanted first."

Jeremy had been getting more and more nervous, but this statement really bugged him. "Exactly *who* wants me?" he complained with sharpening irritation. "And *what* do they want me for? You told me I've been chosen. Okay, so I'm one of these *Ouyperkain* of yours. And I'm not supposed to know any more than that? It's not fair. And I still don't understand why somebody else couldn't get chosen, like Zack, maybe, who knows ten times more than me, or a grown-up. I'm just an ordinary kid, Spider," Jeremy pleaded, his face wrinkling with both resentment and anguish.

The Arkanian went still and quiet, considering carefully, for Jeremy seemed agitated enough to require special handling. A sly, insistent voice began to chirp deep within Jeremy's mind, usurping that silence, like the sound of a small, dark toad hidden beneath a rock.

"Maybe, you are not even an *ordinary* kid, Jeremy," the stealthy voice whispered. "Maybe you are much less—a spine-less coward who is lost without Mommy to hold his hand, feels spiteful toward his little sister, and doesn't have a clue how to be a hero. Maybe, you're going to screw up again, as always, and disappoint everybody."

Jeremy felt a muddy hill of doubt piling up on him, getting deeper with each spadeful of stony accusation that treacher-ous voice shoveled over him. A dark stain of despair spread into his next question.

"What if I can't do it, Alaikin?" he demanded. "What if I'm so useless I can't help anyone?"

The Arkanian answered with a deep, broad melody, a clear stream that lifted Jeremy free and floated him above his mire of doubt.

"You may seem an ordinary boy to yourself, Jeremy, even an inferior one, but this seeming is not who you really are. You, and others yet to be revealed, are *Ouyperkain*, protec-tors of the Cosmic Balance. You have gifts of which you are not yet aware. *Ordúrrg-Zaikh* may whisper doubt to you, for the Dragon prizes Guardians above all other prey, but you must refuse to listen.

"Certainly, you can be harsh and even mean, like anyone, but later you regret it deeply. That is because, however frus-trated and angry, at heart you are kind, gifted with imagina-tion, and moved to love every living being. Even when you fear and hate someone, still you want to do your best for them. Believe *this*, and not your doubts, for it must be true or you would never have welcomed me into your mind and trusted me to take you on this journey."

As Jeremy's gloom faded and his spirits rose, Alaikin's song changed from a smooth, uplifting swell to a brisk, march-like mood. "Earth-traveler," the bright tones rang out, "we are nearing our destination. Though human senses cannot penetrate my force-field, with your gift of imagination you will experience *Tyrdd-cayzh* as we re-enter. In this Time-crunch you'll see everything in your mind's eye. It will be a wild ride, but don't worry—I will keep you safe."

Rising and expanding in warm, golden light, Jeremy felt as if Alaikin had washed away the last of the darkness, the dregs of what must have been the poisonous thoughts of *Ordúrrg-Zaikh* seeping into his mind. He felt happier and luckier than ever before, as if something extraordinary were about to happen. Poised to dive into a pool of glowing gold, he would swim and fly at once through air and water.

Then, *Tyrdd-cayzh* hit. An exploding star of light, white at the core but streaming out in every color of the rainbow, pinwheeled through the black of Space and shrank to a violet shimmer. Planets and stars of all shapes and sizes zoomed in wild twists through uncountable orbits and retraced their paths in the wink of an eye. In the same instant, Jeremy saw his mirror image rush from an immense distance and fuse with a regular image of him. They spun a hundred cartwheels in flaming golden light, then reversed and spun the other way. It all happened at once, both in his mind and, it seemed, outside it, and then, in a flash, it was over.

He found himself standing on solid ground, still dizzy and dazzled. Gone was the golden skin of the Arkanian's force-field, and he could see around him for the first time since leaving Earth. What he saw was disappointing, especially after the intensity of Time-crunch. The air was soft, gray, and thick, like fog but not wet. The ground was the same color, so a few feet away it merged with the air. Staring in any direction, Jeremy could see only gray murk.

He'd gotten used to being wrapped in Alaikin's golden energy, but he couldn't adjust to this gray wall pressing in from every side. Lost on an alien planet, he waited for something horrible to stalk out of the mist. "Alaikin?" he thought, with rising panic. There was no reply. "Spider?" he shouted, trembling, but the thick air sucked up sounds like a sponge. "Where are you?" he screamed.

Cleo wriggled and mewed in his arms, for he'd forgotten her and squeezed when he yelled. The little cat sniffed the air and peered around curiously, twitching her tail. Jeremy petted her and felt a little calmer, for she didn't seem at all alarmed. He lifted her up to face him, nose to nose. The Arkanian's force field had left her, too: the green-gold light in her eyes was all her own.

"Cleo," Jeremy whispered, "Alaikin wouldn't leave us, would he, all alone with no way home?" The cat tried to twist free, and not wanting to lose his last friend, Jeremy brought her back down and cradled her in his arms again.

He was afraid of getting lost almost as much as he hated fighting. Once, when he was about six years old, he'd taken his skateboard several blocks farther from home than ever before. Excitement tingled through his body like dancing sunlight, but when he forgot the way back that wonderful sensation merged into a terror like sudden, pelting hail. A kind old man found him frozen still on the sidewalk, tears streaming down his face, and took him back home.

Jeremy was grateful, but his shame about getting lost in the first place, and even worse, breaking down in tears, burned hot in his face. He didn't even thank the old man, but quickly slipped from his guiding hand and ducked into a familiar alley. After this, Jeremy had avoided exploring any place he hadn't first visited with his parents or Gramps, until he and Zack became explorers together.

When Cleo stirred again in Jeremy's arms and mewed curiously, he realized that he'd been lost in memory and hadn't moved for minutes. Now he glanced down at her, and perhaps imagined—for hadn't the Arkanian said he had imagination?—that Cleo smiled and nodded, as if she understood his fear. Then a familiar melody sounded softly in his mind.

"Alaikin!" Jeremy shouted, "Am I ever glad you're back!" Jeremy was so happy that he forgot his misery, but at the same time he was ashamed of his happiness because it showed how down he'd actually been—so he tried to disguise it. "Not that we weren't doing okay, Cleo and I, but we just weren't sure which way to go," he quickly added. He sensed that the Arkanian saw right through this bluff, but was too polite to expose it.

"Sorry," Alaikin sang, "I needed a few moments to gather myself. I'm not far off. Just put Cleo down and follow her to me. She'll follow her nose."

Cleo yawned, arched her back in a huge stretch, and padded in a circle around Jeremy, peering and sniffing. Then she stalked off briskly to his left, her tail raised like a flag for him to follow. He took a step and nearly keeled over: both his legs seemed to have fallen asleep.

"Careful, Jeremy," the Arkanian warned. "You're not quite over *Tyrdd-cayzh*. It's as if you've been on a long sea voyage and need to get your land legs again. There! Now you're okay. Go ahead, pick up Cleo again."

As Jeremy lifted the cat, she burst into a roaring purr. It was the nicest sound he'd heard since leaving Earth. He followed her gaze to the Arkanian, who rested in a web floating a few feet above them, not attached to anything.

"Where are we, Alaikin?" Jeremy asked. "It's really weird: you can't see a thing."

"Welcome to the center of the universe," sang the Arkanian. "If you don't mind, I'll hitch a ride with you, and we can get over this last bit in no time. You'll want to put Cleo down again: she could do with some exercise."

A strand shot from one of Alaikin's forelegs, wrapped around Jeremy's wrist, and held. "Bull's eye," the Arkanian chortled. With another leg, it pointed out into the curtain of gray. "Left march, Jeremy, toward that patch over there."

"What patch?" Jeremy exclaimed. "It's all the same. How will we find anything in this?"

"Don't you see it's a bit lighter over there? No? Ah, I forget human eyes have limitations. Well then, you'll have to follow

Cleo. She seems to know exactly where to go. I'd hitch onto her tail, but she twitches it so much I'd get airsick.

"That's it, we're coming along fine. Stop swinging your arm, please. I don't care to bob about like a balloon. Onward! Do you see that clearing?"

"It *is* getting lighter," Jeremy said happily. "Why is it all gray like this, anyway? It's not natural."

"What a sensible Earth-child! Perfectly true, it is not natural. It's what *you* would call camouflage. After all, we can't have just anybody knocking about the center of the universe. Need to make it difficult to locate for certain parties who don't have the best intentions. You should know by now, Jeremy, some very dark forces lurk in this cosmos."

"But how does all the gray get here? It doesn't just happen by itself, does it?"

"Right again. It comes from the *Zhystrém Haistrál*—the Flowering Crystal."

"The *what*? Alaikin, that's impossible. Even in English, crystals don't flower!"

"What an absurd Earth-child! An hour ago, Earth-time, you thought I was impossible, yet here we are chatting pleasantly at the center of the universe. Oh, don't look so glum. After all, you really can't help it—you behave like a typical Earth-sort. Won't believe anything unless your nose is rubbed in it. Well, if you don't think that a crystal can flower, see for yourself!"

Cleo had prowled on into the gray. Jeremy followed a few steps in the cat's direction. A vast, electric blue space opened around him, as if he'd flown above the clouds in an airplane. The brightness dazzled until his eyes adjusted.

In mid-air hovered an enormous rose, a single perfect blossom. Its color cycled through every hue in the rainbow: red, orange, yellow, green, blue, violet, and then again. As the colors changed, so did the odor, from mildly sweet pink to spicy orange, lemony yellow, pine green, and deep purple musk. Jeremy walked on in a daze. As he approached the bottom

49

petals, each hovering a few feet above the ground and larger than his mattress, he saw that they were not made of ordinary flower stuff. Each petal contained countless little pyramid-shaped crystals, glowing with the shifting colors that drenched his eyes.

"Alaikin," Jeremy murmured, "it's *so* beautiful! You never told me about this."

"It's too beautiful for words," the Arkanian replied. "You wouldn't have believed me if I'd tried."

Suddenly, a bee about a quarter the size of a football zoomed straight at Jeremy's face. He ducked, while Cleopatra let out a short yowl and chased the creature until it disappeared into the curtain of gray.

"What the heck was that?" Jeremy asked.

"Crystal bee," Alaikin replied, his melodious chuckle singing in Jeremy's mind. And then Jeremy noticed hordes of the bee creatures dancing around the *Zhystrém Haistrál,* all changing color as the huge flower did. Like living bits of rainbow, some of the crystal bees zoomed off into the gray, from which others returned.

"They don't sting, do they," Jeremy asked doubtfully, entranced by their beauty but wary, as usual, of any possible source of pain.

"No," Alaikin replied, "where you'd expect to find a stinger they have something like a fine brush sprinkled with droplets of a potion so powerful that it can heal nearly any injury short of death itself. That is the distilled power of the *Zhystrém Haistrál.*"

"Wow," Jeremy responded, "my dad could use some of that for his patients. But Alaikin, why are there bees when there aren't any other flowers for them to carry pollen to?"

"That would be a sensible question on Earth," the Arkanian answered, "where bees help fertilize so many flowers, but here things are different. There is only the *Zhystrém Haistrál,* one flower, and the bees gather pollen from it and bring it to the gray zone. There, most of it grows into more gray, thickening the mist that protects the Flower. But some special bees change a few grains of pollen into an amber fluid that looks and behaves much like honey—it crystallizes when dried out. The bees bring these new crystals back to the Flower, and that is how the *Zhystrém Haistrál* grows."

Cleo gave up stalking the bee that had disappeared into the gray. The little cat sniffed one last time, turned on her heels, and marched back to Jeremy with her tail held high and her nose in the air. Jeremy laughed, for this was the same queenly dignity she displayed when a mouse got away—as if it hadn't been worth catching in the first place.

Alaikin called Jeremy back to himself. "Time is pressing," the Arkanian sang gently. "Within the *Zhystrém Haistrál* is the knowledge you need, and to get this knowledge you must merge with the Flower. Lie down on one of the petals and it will take you in."

Jeremy stared at the enormous bloom, surrounded by dancing bees. The thought of being swallowed by that hugeness made him gulp. He felt an all too familiar trembling sensation crawling like a centipede from his belly up his spine. Would he never stop being so scared when he had to do something new or difficult? "Can't you come too, Alaikin?" he pleaded.

"I'm afraid not, Jeremy. I have brought you here, as I have brought other Guardians, but at the center of the universe each *Ouyperkai* must find his or her path alone. Whatever your doubts, know that you can succeed in this task, and many more that you will face. Now don't be frightened: I promise you will come out the same as you go in—except for new memories and more wisdom. Quickly now, the *Zhystrém Haistrál* awaits."

Jeremy lifted himself onto a lower petal. It rocked slightly, or was that his arms shaking? It's easy enough for Alaikin to tell *me* not to be scared, Jeremy thought. He doesn't have to go in here!

The Flowering Crystal felt cool, dry, and—somehow—spongy rather than sharp and hard against his hands and knees. He crawled to the center of the huge petal and lay on his back. After a moment, the petal trembled into motion, its sides curling up over him and then folding down toward his face. He held his breath and thrust out his arms in a cold panic, ready to fight smothering weight. But his fear melted into pliant warmth when the petal came down light as a blanket of feathers.

The colors of the *Zhystrém Haistrál* grew rich and thick, pressing in until they seemed to soak right through him. He heard wonderful music, like the Arkanian's haunting song but wilder and deeper, more varied in tone, a symphony rather than a violin solo. Feeling very much like a flower himself, with color and sound pulsing through him like blood and thought, Jeremy waited.

7 VISIONS

At first, the colors of the Flowering Crystal swirled through Jeremy's mind like hues of every lovely sunset he'd ever watched. Then they shaped themselves into a scene so real that he gasped with astonishment. Grandpa Heinrich sat at his roll-top desk, leafing through pages of pictures and whirling, elegant script like intricate music. Jeremy longed to sit beside him and re-live history as they once had, translating the script he guessed must be in the Primal Tongue. But—how frustrating!—this was impossible.

Though Grandpa Heinrich seemed alive, he was only an image, like a character in a 3-D movie or a hologram. The Flowering Crystal was replaying the past, perhaps within Jeremy's own brain, for as he lay enfolded in the petal he had no idea whether he was watching some sort of screen or seeing things in his mind, as in imagination or dreams. He was grateful to the Crystal for bringing his grandfather back to him, but terribly sad and more than a little angry that he could not actually be with him.

Wreathed in smoke, Grandpa Heinrich pored over his book, while a rainstorm thrashed the trees outside. In the lightning's flashes, the pictures came to life, a panorama of history passing before Jeremy's eyes: royalty, nobles, and priests in lavish garments; peasants and workers in smocks and rags; caped merchants and travelers voyaging in caravans and aboard ships, on horseback and camelback, or slogging through mud or snow on foot.

Jeremy witnessed Olympics and tournaments; pagan and Christian holidays; the smoke of animal sacrifices blending with the smoke of incense; armies marching and herders tending their flocks; artists painting on ceramics, canvas, and paper; streams of wild geese migrating through the cycles of years.

All human life seemed to spill out of the book and into the eyes and mind of Grandpa Heinrich, and Jeremy as well, floating in a trance on great waves of time and history. But Grandpa Heinrich seemed anything but carried away: as each page turned, he narrowed his eyes and examined the scene before him, searching closely.

In a garden fragrant with blossoms, beside wandering streams channeled through angular black rocks and white crystal clusters, elegant, happy people drank, danced, and conversed. Grandpa Heinrich lingered over this page, and Jeremy would have guessed that he was enjoying the scene as much as its participants if not for the worry lines that raked his forehead, the hard set of his lips as he gazed down at the page, and his sudden cry of alarm.

As his grandfather drew back and stood, staring at the page, Jeremy too saw the splash of red at the top. He watched it stretch out and penetrate downward, splitting the picture, a menacing rivulet of blood. The red strand spread and shaped itself until both Jeremy and his grandfather gasped with recognition. Across the page, splintering the once tranquil garden, thrashed a vicious red worm, and all the figures it contacted began to ravage the others, snapping and slashing like rabid dogs.

Grandpa Heinrich lurched back from his desk and either fell or braced himself against the bookcase along back wall of his apartment. A shower of volumes bounced off his shoulders and, like dead birds, thudded splayed to the ground. At that moment, Jeremy felt everything his grandfather did. Strength rose in his body, and with a weak but steady voice he chanted an ancient spell until a brutal shudder racked him.

As Grandpa Heinrich fell to the floor and lay still, Jeremy felt grief tear at him like a hook in a fish, but alongside his pain he felt what his grandfather did: his body dwindle and fall away, leaving his mind to float still and at peace in vast black space. In the book, the red worm was also still: it had stopped writhing and slowly faded from the page. Then light flooded Jeremy's awareness. Amazed, he found himself still alive, stunned but cushioned in the bright softness of the *Zhystrém Haistrál.*

A voice sounded in Jeremy's mind, a crystalline voice like the tones of many wind-chimes. "Your grandfather was *Brÿle Ouyperkai,* the last Great Guardian of his generation," said the Flowering Crystal. "He knew that the Time of Unbalance had come and that he was too old to defeat the Enemy. Yet, when he saw the *Zaikhthréem* invade the life within the Great Book, he still fought. He stopped the Dragon Spawn by chanting the Spell of Isis and forced them from your world, but only for a time, and at the cost of his life. *Ordúrrg-Zaikh* went on seeking entry to Earth."

"So, that thing Zack and Sandy and I saw in the microscope was the same as the one in the picture," Jeremy thought. "Both of them Dragon Spawn. *Zaikhthréem.* Horrible things! But the one in the scope didn't get out, and Grandpa stopped the other one—so everything is okay, right?"

"Watch!" the crystalline voice commanded.

A new vision formed in Jeremy's mind. There was Zack, bent over his microscope. Sandy stood behind him, and beside her Jeremy saw himself. "It already happened," he thought. "I was there." But this time Jeremy saw, through Zack's eye, what he couldn't before. The red worm tore loose from the droplet and flashed up through the barrel of the microscope. As if in an x-ray, it snaked through Zack's eye and buried itself in his brain. Zack turned from the scope and snarled at Sandy, his eyes glaring red. And then the scene changed again.

Sara lay on the sofa, whispering to herself, but now what she said made sense, for a red swarm seethed around her.

"Grandpa," she pleaded, "come back. Red wigglers are hurting me. Make them go away."

"She is *Kailáeria*, a Sensitive," said the crystalline voice. "The *Zaikhthréem* have not been able to invade her yet because she is so very loving, but so keenly does she feel the Unbalance that her mind is unbalanced too." Then Jeremy entered Sara's mind, saw through her eyes, and felt her terror, far worse than any he had ever known.

A maddening jumble of noise and pictures whirled through her head, like a TV at max volume switching endlessly from one channel to another. She saw the visions Jeremy had witnessed in Alaikin's mirror: animals running from whirling flames, the bleeding people of the ruined city searching through wreckage. Red lightning flickered as the Spawn writhed across the pictures in a roar of Dragon laughter. Jeremy felt Aunt Lillian's cool hand on Sara's forehead. Was it he or Sara whimpering, "Grandpa, come back!"

"Poor Sara," Jeremy thought. "She's only a little girl. Why does she have to see all that stuff?"

"She sees the future for which *Ordúrrg-Zaikh* hungers so fiercely," the Flowering Crystal answered, "one of war and destruction. This is not the only future, but it will happen unless new Guardians oppose the Dragon. Will you be a Guardian, Jeremy? Will you number among the *Ouyperkain*?"

A sly, toad voice edged into Jeremy's mind, but this time its familiar chirps quickly merged and revved into a shriek like feedback from a powerful microphone. All the doubts and fears he'd ever felt screamed through him like a jet of filthy water carrying sharp-edged rocks, spinning and tearing him helplessly. Beaten down and gashed, he heard another voice just as he was sure he was dying. In the chiming tones of *Zhystrém Haistrál* came a song of beauty so vast that it seemed to surround and absorb the shrill pounding he suffered.

Child of love and imagination,
These gifts will not betray
But block the Dragon's malice
That makes the Balance sway.

Hard trials you will face
And your path has just begun,
But at last you'll win the race
And peace when all is done.

Like a breath of sweet, healing air, the melody closed Jeremy's inner wounds, filled his lungs with oxygen, and charged him with new confidence. The flood of doubt ebbed away, and with it the chaos that had scrambled his mind.

"Will you be *Ouyperkai?*" the Flowering Crystal asked again.

"Yes," Jeremy answered, and the thought was small but solid in the great surrounding silence. There! He'd said it, and now he hoped the *Zhystrém Haistrál* would let him go. But that hope faded when its next utterance again filled him with dread.

"Welcome, Jeremy the Guardian," the Flowering Crystal said, "to the battle for Earth. Know that it was not by chance that the *Zaikhthréem* infected your best friend. It was *you* the Spawn wanted most, but unknown to yourself you already had the qualities of a Guardian, so you were difficult prey. In Zack, it found a flaw that gave it easier entry to your world, and a path to you. The *Zaikhthréem* do the will of the Great Dragon, who will never stop trying to possess you. And now you must meet and know your enemy fully, so it will never deceive you again."

Once more, he found himself at the entrance to the dark cave, his skin crawling with the vile laughter of *Ordúrrg-Zaikh.* Pushed by some stubborn force, he was drawn deeper and deeper into the cave, choking on the ammonia fumes of the beast's breath and beaten by the powerful fist of its heart. Then, at the back of the lair, he saw it.

A gigantic eye covered with a smear of slime bulged out like a monstrous red yolk, its bloody light glaring off the black scales of the Dragon's reptilian body and blazing into the dark space of the cave. Slowly, the eye turned full on Jeremy. Within it, thousands of red Spawn sparked like lightning. How could creatures as tiny as Alaikin and he defeat something so gigantic and malevolent?

Suddenly, one hideous worm pulsed to the surface, burst out, streaked toward him, and hovered in front of his face. As its foul odor washed over him, his insides curdled with hatred and greed. Let his enemies beware, for never again would anyone shame or frighten him. Nothing would stop him from getting what he wanted. He was immensely strong, and his heart was huge and hot and cruel enough to conquer everything. He would rip and crush his way through the world until he became King Jeremy, richest of all, Emperor of Everyone. Wild laughter tore from his throat. He opened his mouth and roared out his rage and power.

The lidless eye of *Ordúrrg-Zaikh* rolled slowly as its great, gloating voice boomed in the cave. "Who would oppose Me, when I offer eternal triumph?"

But as the beast's challenge echoed hollowly, from the whirlpool of his rage, Jeremy heard Sara's small voice, thin and frightened. "Help, Jeremy!" she cried, "Red wigglers are hurting me. Come back, please!" Then he saw her as if she were standing beside him, looking into his eyes. He reached out and touched her face, and she was gone, but the wet of her tears still cooled his palm. His waking nightmare faded and he was himself again, but filled with a new, sea-deep calm.

"Who would oppose Me?" the Dragon thundered once more, blasting the cave with flaming waves of sound.

"Hear me, *Ordúrrg-Zaikh,*" Jeremy thought quietly, "I oppose you." And his thought held like steel against the waves.

The beast stirred its vast black bulk and reared up, but in that moment Jeremy found himself wrapped again in the shifting colors of the *Zhystrém Haistrál*.

"Now you know the power of *Ordúrrg-Zaikh*," the Flower's voice chimed. "Fear and greed: these are its weapons. All beings know them, and react in two ways. The way of the Dragon, anger and hate, feeds a quest for power that, without love, leads to ruin. But the Arkanians' way, love and caring, leads to true power that nurtures and restores the Cosmic Balance. Know this, Jeremy of Earth, and choose the right path, for only this wisdom will defeat the Dragon. The Beast has seen you, and you have seen the *Zaikhthréem* go forth to infect the worlds. Beware, for now they will seek you."

"Why did Zack get infected?" Jeremy thought. "What was the flaw that let in the Spawn?"

"Your friend was a loving being who wanted to use his knowledge to help others, but his greed for success grew so strong that he resented anyone he thought stood in his way. As that became nearly everyone, a seed of hatred took root in him. It has grown into a sapling nurtured by *Ordúrrg-Zaikh*, who promises everything but delivers nothing. Zack is now in grave danger, but the tree of hate is not full grown and the love that was in him is there still. Your constant friendship may win him back, but beware, for he will try to win you to *Ordúrrg-Zaikh* at every chance."

"What happens next?" Jeremy thought.

"You have seen terrible things," the Flowering Crystal answered, "but now let me show you something pleasant. Then, you will know what to do next."

In an instant, Jeremy found himself sitting as he once had at Grandpa Heinrich's massive oak desk, with the great golden book open before him. The pages turned, picture followed picture, and again all history unrolled before his eyes. Men and women lived, worked, and laughed. Myriad animals roamed through jungle, desert, and ocean. Ancient villages grew, thrived, and decayed as the ages passed, until at last they lay buried and forgotten beneath modern cities. The endless river of history rolled on and on, until Jeremy became dizzy with wonder and happiness. At last the vision faded, and the voice of the *Zhystrém Haistrál* chimed again.

"The book is named *Shaiféir al Shehn, The Book of Life*, and it is the seed of all that lives on your planet. If the Balance is set right, this seed will grow into a future like a brilliant flower. But if the Dragon has its way, the *Shaiféir al Shehn* will wither and crumble into nothing. You must find this book, for in it is the secret that will drive back the *Zaikhthréem* and right the Balance. *Ordúrrhg-Zaikh* will oppose you at every step, and time grows short. But that is your task, Jeremy of Earth—to restore the Balance—as that is the task of all *Ouyperkain*."

The voice of the Flowering Crystal fell silent. The huge petal on which Jeremy lay trembled and unfolded. He slid to the ground, his legs shaking so much that he could barely stand. Searching the dazzling blue space around the Flower, he saw no one. A crystal bee zoomed past, and then something rubbed against his calves. "Cleo!" he shouted, lifting the purring cat into his arms. "Am I glad to see you! But where's Alaikin?"

"Being jerked around like a feather in a storm," the Arkanian sang grumpily. Alaikin floated in a web a few feet above Jeremy's head, anchored by a strand to Cleopatra's swishing tail. "Just when I finally get her to curl up and lie still, you show up and the bouncing starts again. Stop grinning! After all, I couldn't hitch myself to the center of the universe. Quite against the rules unless invited, and I wasn't."

The Arkanian shot a strand down to Jeremy's arm and reeled in the one attached to Cleo. "You're not exactly a smooth ride, Jeremy, but anything would be better than that twitchy tail. Well, where to now?"

"Don't you know?" Jeremy asked in astonishment.

"How would I?" Alaikin replied. "I don't listen in on other people's conversations unless invited. You're the leader now.

I'll be only a sort of interstellar omnibus from here on. But what is that glowing in your pocket? A gift from the *Zhystrém Haistrál?*"

Jeremy reached into his side pants pocket, felt something warm, and pulled out the ankh. It shimmered with light that changed color in time with the Flowering Crystal.

"I expect that will have all sorts of uses," Alaikin said, "though you'll never know until you need them. That is how the *Zhystrém Haistrál* works, so as to keep its gifts from uses it wouldn't approve. But you haven't answered my question. Where to? I'd love to find something stable to attach to, and this light is giving me what you Earth-sorts might call a migraine."

"We have to get back to Earth as fast as we can," Jeremy replied. "I've got to find—"

"Never mind, don't tell me what you must do. I was not chosen to hear it, so I need not know it. Whatever it is, you must do yourself: that's the way with assignments from the *Zhystrém Haistrál*. To Earth, then. But you've endured a great deal in a short while, and you look worn out. Let's make a quick rest stop to pick up your spirits. Ready?"

Jeremy hesitated because, given his experiences with Alaikin so far, he wondered just how restful the "rest stop" would be. The best he could do was a reluctant half nod, but that was enough for the Spider.

"Then all aboard for Arkania," he heard, as the golden sphere began its descent to his eye.

8 BITTER AND SWEET

Jeremy lay in the flower-filled meadow he'd seen in Alaikin's mirror. Above fluttered two yellow butterflies with brown tiger's-eye spotted wings. The warm breeze carried scents of grass and lemon blossom. Cleo stirred in his arms, glanced sleepily at the butterflies, and closed her eyes again. Jeremy gazed at a mild blue sky lined with feathery wings of cloud. He felt so lazy and happy that he never wanted to get up again.

"Arkania is alright!" he thought drowsily. "Alaikin sure is lucky to live here."

Soft footsteps approached. The two honey-furred creatures gazed down, golden eyes wide and wondering. They were bigger than Jeremy, almost as big as grown people, but they moved so gently that when they reached down he was not afraid. Caring hands lifted and held him while he got his balance.

Cleo mewed, jumped down into the grass, and sniffed at one of the creatures, inspecting it carefully. Satisfied, she lifted her tail high and rubbed against its legs, purring in her most inviting voice. When the furry creature stroked her head, she flopped over and wriggled in the grass.

"They must have cats on Arkania," Jeremy thought, as the creature stroked Cleo's belly. She closed her eyes and purred in pure happiness. The second creature joined in and soon they made a game of petting, inventing new strokes each of which Cleo loved more than the last. She wriggled and purred so deliriously that Jeremy thought she would float up into the air.

"Cleo thinks she's in Cat Heaven," sang Alaikin, "and my co-beings are delighted to have found a new life form."

Jeremy searched the flowery meadow until he found Alaikin dangling from a sunflower. "What kind of creature are they?" he asked.

"This life-form is called *Meilixchroumistrai*," Alaikin answered, "though they will not be offended if you call them *melis* for short. They are different from me, but once I looked like them and someday they will be like me."

"I'm glad they like their short name, because the long one is a jaw-breaker," Jeremy said. "But you're talking in riddles again. What did you mean before, about co-beings?"

"*Anhörin* in the Primal Tongue, Alaikin answered. All life on Arkania is one. We take many different forms, but in essence, in our source energy, we are the same. Where do your Earth butterflies come from, Jeremy?"

"I guess they come from eggs."

"Yes," Alaikin sang, "but that is only the beginning. The egg becomes a caterpillar, which in turn spins a cocoon around itself. There it lies until, when the time comes, a butterfly emerges. Each Arkanian changes form like your caterpillars, or like tadpoles that become frogs. But we have many more forms than your creatures. Once an Arkanian is ready for the change, it goes into a deep sleep, and awakens as any one of a million types of *anhörin*."

"Metamorphosis," Jeremy murmured. "That's what it's called when an animal changes so completely."

"Yes," replied Alaikin, "that is the English word for changing forms. It is *shaernourddhí* in the Primal Tongue, but for us the process is different. There is no final form for an Arkanian. A butterfly dies a butterfly, but in *shaernourddhí* we change and go on living, and then we change again, and again—always the same and always different."

Jeremy was quiet. A thought took shape in his mind, a bud opening into a flower. He was happy because it was a beautiful thought, but he was sad because it might be true only for Arkanian *anhörin.*

"Then nothing ever really dies on Arkania?" Jeremy asked, "like it does on Earth? My grandpa told me that the ancient people thought we came back in a different form after death. Reincarnation, they called it, but Gramps didn't know if it was true."

The Arkanian's music welled up in Jeremy's mind, sad but beautiful, just as his thought had been. "It is true, Jeremy, that we Arkanians do not die as Earth-ones do. When we have changed through all anhörin, we return to the Energy from which we came—but that is not death, because we were born there. Many Earth-ones believe in reincarnation, although it has not been accepted by everyone because very few remember past lives. But past anhörin are as real as present ones for all Arkanians, and we can see and touch our source Energy. You will witness this before we leave this planet."

"It sounds like being an Arkanian is a real picnic," Jeremy sighed, "a permanent vacation."

"Ah, yes," Alaikin answered. "It is pleasant to be an Arkanian. But it is not always pleasant to bear our responsibilities. For we are *Ouyperkain* of all living worlds, and your Earth—as you would say—is no picnic."

The two *melis* had stopped petting Cleo and gazed silently down at Alaikin, their golden eyes twinkling in the sunlight.

"If they are like you," Jeremy asked, "why don't they talk or share minds with me? All they've done is pet Cleo and play."

"Arkanians share the same Energy whatever form they take," Alaikin answered, "but otherwise they are different. I am a musical and mindful form, so I communicate by melody and thought. *Melis* are a playful form, so they communicate by play. If you want to get to know *melis*, you must play with them."

"What kind of games do they play?" Jeremy asked.

Alaikin answered with his little musical chuckle. "Oh, nothing special. They just play."

One of the *melis* had been picking a bunch of flowers while Jeremy and Alaikin were sharing minds. Suddenly it threw the blossoms in Jeremy's face. As the soft petals pelted his skin, he smelled a wonderful scent, wild and spicy and sweet. Without thinking, he grabbed a bunch of flowers and flung them back at the *meli*.

In an instant, he was tumbling in the grass, giggling and scrambling with both *melis*, who chased him in turn. It was like a game of tag in which the object was not to run away but to get caught. Over and over they rolled, and Cleopatra joined in, her soft paws batting at Jeremy and his new friends.

Jeremy had always wondered how Cleo felt when she went wild with catnip, and now he knew. Bubbling happiness washed away all of his troubles and left no thought but to play and play forever. At last, too tired to move, he lay with his head on the shoulder of one of the *melis*, snuggling in its soft, tawny fur. Cleo curled up on his stomach while he caught his breath and gazed up at the golden light streaming through the blue Arkanian sky.

A large green bird suddenly wheeled in its flight and came straight at Jeremy. It had red patches under its wings and the yellow on its back glowed in the sunlight. Cleopatra leapt away as the bird loomed close, but before Jeremy could move, the creature landed on his bent knee and peered down into his face.

"It's a parrot!" he shouted, trying to scuttle away on his back, like a turned-over crab. That didn't work, for the bird still perched calmly on his knee, and the knee went with him as he crawled backward. The big bird blinked and looked at him sideways out of one glinting golden eye.

"Don't let it bite me, Alaikin!" Jeremy yelled. "Can't you make it go away?"

"No, I'm afraid I can't," Alaikin sang, his melody bouncing with laughter. "But it won't bite as long as you talk to it. In fact, this *baibaidínn* will insist on conversation, for it is our most talkative life-form. You'd better greet it."

"Hello!" Jeremy said timidly.

"Hello, how are you?" the bird answered. Jeremy was surprised that its voice was not gruff and raspy, like the parrots he'd heard in pet shops, but low and mellow, like a clarinet.

"You look like a parrot," he said doubtfully. "How come you don't sound like one?"

The bird ruffled its feathers, flared its tail, and hunched its shoulders so it looked even bigger. Because its eyes were on the sides of its head, it couldn't look at Jeremy with both at once. First one surly eye examined him and then the other.

"Get this straight, Earth-punk," the bird suddenly snapped. "You are addressing a Greater *Baibaidínn*, and don't you forget it. I've just been stuck in a cage for nine Earth-years pretending to be a parrot for an old lady who watched TV day and night. 'Pretty bird, pretty bird'—yechhh! You can't imagine how boring it was: I started to sound like a TV. And you—now that I'm finally free—you want me be a parrot again? All right, you asked for it. Awwk!" the bird screamed in Jeremy's face. "Cracker! Polly wanna cracker! More news at eleven. Awwwwk!"

"Oh no," Jeremy said quickly, covering his ears. "No, Mr. *Baibaidínn*, please don't be a parrot."

"All right then," the big bird continued in its mellow voice. "I won't. But don't be surprised if I slip. What do you expect, after nine years of parrot-hood?"

The *baibaidínn* stood on one leg and scratched the feathers of its neck with the other. "You have some nasty little fleas on Earth, too," it said testily. "Life there has become very unpleasant lately. I was a cheerful creature before this last trip, but now I'm so grouchy I'd as soon bite you as talk to you. Awwwwwwk!" the bird screamed again, hunching its shoulders and glaring ferociously. "Technical problems, please stay tuned."

Jeremy flinched and scuttled backward. "Whoops, I am sorry!" said the baibaidínn. "It happens when I'm upset. Please, help me break these nasty parrot habits."

The bird humbly lowered its head, but Jeremy still detected a wicked gleam in its eye. "I don't believe that bird is as sorry as it pretends," he thought, hoping the *baibaidínn* couldn't read his mind. He decided to give the bird something to talk about before it could use its powerful beak for nastier purposes. "*Baibaidínn*," he asked gently, "why were you on Earth, anyway? Do Arkanians come to Earth all the time?"

"Of course," the *baibaidínn* responded. "We Arkanians are *Ouyperkain Orthein*, Guardians of Earth, so we have to keep an eye on you." The bird stared at Jeremy with one eye, its pupil contracting and expanding as it spoke, which made him feel dizzy.

"Usually," the *baibaidínn* continued, "we send flesh-forms that resemble Earth creatures, so you don't get hostile. Long ago, Earth-ones mind-shared and spoke with all of our forms, but now they react badly to anything unfamiliar. On this assignment, I was peacefully flying through the jungle, enjoying the morning sun, when I got caught in a net. Next thing I was stuck in the old lady's cage. What an awful life," the bird moaned, hunching and menacing again. "What a simply aw-wwwwwk-ful life. Over to you now, over to you."

"You're doing it again," Jeremy said in a soothing tone. "Acting like a parrot."

Cleopatra, curiosity overcoming caution, padded to Jeremy's side. She sat regally, tail wrapped around her, studying the *baibaidínn*, whose pupil got huge and then contracted suspiciously.

"That cat," said the *baibaidínn*, "remembers my visits in ancient times. They seldom let on, but cats remember everything that ever happened to their kind." Cleo stretched and yawned, opening her mouth wide, which the bird took the wrong way. "Awwwwk!" it screamed, stabbing the air with its beak. "Enemy alien, phasers on stun!"

Calming down again, the *baibaidínn* watched Cleo closely with one eye while searching the ground with the other. "Down there," it said, motioning with its beak, "is another form that visits Earth."

A large horned beetle was crawling through the grass. Cleopatra went down on her belly and silently crept up on the creature. When Jeremy grabbed her, she shot him a very offended look.

He was remembering his grandfather again, opening a book of paintings from the Egyptian tombs. "You see this beetle with horns?" Grandpa Heinrich had said. "The Egyptians called it the scarab and thought it was a spirit guide for their journey to heaven. It must be true! My scarab ring is guiding my hand to a chocolate bar in the drawer. Heaven!"

For the first time on Arkania, Jeremy felt sad. He missed Mom and Dad and even Sara, as difficult as she had become, and he wanted to go home. Alaikin had been dangling quietly from the sunflower, but now the alien's words sang softly in Jeremy's mind.

"Your grandfather's death was sad not only for you, Jeremy, but for your entire world. You see, we Arkanians cannot always be on Earth. When the power of *Ordúrrg-Zaikh* is greater on another world, we must concentrate our forces there. While we are away, we find a few Earth-ones to be *Ouyperkain Orthein* until we return. We teach them to watch for *Ordúrrg-Zaikh*, and to call us if its power becomes too great."

"Grandpa was a *Ouyperkai,* wasn't he?" Jeremy asked.

"Yes," the Arkanian answered, "he was a great one, *Brýle-Ouyperkai,* and in his last years he was one of very few. We did not expect *Ordúrrg-Zaikh* to attack Earth with so much power, for we had just won a great victory over it on another world."

"Your grandfather was a brave man," the *baibaidínn* added kindly, sharing minds with both Alaikin and Jeremy, "but he was alone and caught by surprise. Still, he managed to beat back the swarming *zaikthréem* and call for us before he died. The signal was weak, but we heard it, we came, and we found you."

"Alaikin," Jeremy asked, "What do Arkanians actually do on Earth? I mean, did they build the Pyramids or win World War II or stuff like that?"

"No, Jeremy, we cannot interfere with the worlds we guard. They must fight the battle themselves. We never actually *do* anything. Our task is to help Earth-ones recognize the Dragon in themselves and others, and learn how to oppose it. As you are discovering, far more is required than blind force. *Ordúrrg-Zaikh* is cunning, and co-opts anyone who is both powerful and ignorant. The Earth-born must discover this by themselves, for only then can they carry into battle the shield of wisdom that wards off self-deception, so unsheathing the sword of courage."

Jeremy lay on his back, silently gazing at the sky. He hardly knew what Alaikin meant by this high-flown language, and he didn't care enough to figure it out. He felt as lonely and miserable as he could ever remember. All the doubts that had melted away in the Flowering Crystal and playing with the *melis* were back.

How could anyone expect him to fight *Ordúrrg-Zaikh*, even with help from other *Ouyperkain*? He'd always been afraid of fighting anybody, and when bullies challenged him he tried to wiggle out of it. He was, he thought sadly, a coward, a wuss, or not much better. If *Ordúrrg-Zaikh* could kill a man as smart and brave as Grandpa Heinrich, what would it do to a chicken like him? It was no fair, no fair at all.

Alaikin's music played softly in Jeremy's mind, but he was sick and tired of listening. He only wanted to get away, far away. He jumped up and began to run, forgetting the *baibaidínn* still perched on his knee. "Awwwwk!" the bird screamed, flapping its wings. "Losing altitude, bail out!" But Jeremy paid no attention, for now he was sprinting across the meadow, headed no place special—just away.

He ran out of breath near a grove of flowering lemon trees and threw himself down on the grassy turf. As he gasped for air, tears got into his nose and sobs choked him. Yet even in his misery he noticed that the sky was darkening, not with night-black but with a deep, rich blue. A raspy tongue licked his ear: Cleopatra was feasting on the salt of his tears. Jeremy grabbed her and hugged her so hard that she flattened her ears and tried to wriggle away. "Cleo!" he sobbed, "don't run away. You're my only friend in the whole world."

That was not exactly true. The two *melis* bounded up, and each threw flowers in Jeremy's face. "No!" he shouted "I don't want to play!" The *melis* stared at him for one bewildered moment and then stood on their hands and threw flowers with their feet.

Jeremy started laughing—they looked so silly he couldn't help it. Then the *baibaidínn* flew up towing Alaikin and landed in a lemon tree, swinging the Spider violently back and forth and making its music lurch like a broken-down merry-go-round's. Jeremy could only laugh harder.

"I say," he voiced inwardly, making fun of Alaikin's English accent, "terribly talented of you. Spot of rodeo, what? If you could ride a bronc as well as that *baibaidínn*, you'd take first prize!"

"Do be quiet, Earth-brat," Alaikin's voice wobbled. "You're as English as an Iowa farmer, and I'm too airsick to be amused."

"Stop complaining," said the *baibaidínn*, hunching its shoulders and peering at Alaikin with one clever eye. "It's you who's upset the child with all your philosophy."

"You'd both better stop arguing and start thinking about staying dry," Jeremy said, still laughing. "We're in for a storm." The sky was now deep violet, and clouds were gathering. The breeze fell and the air became dead calm.

The Arkanians seemed to soak up the silence. Alaikin dangled from a branch, glinting in a last ray of sunlight that escaped between the clouds. When the Arkanian's words finally sounded in Jeremy's mind, they gleamed with solemn, silvery melody. The sound was close, yet somehow distant too, like a tone struck on the bell of endless Space.

"Yes, Jeremy," Alaikin sang, "there will be a storm—a special one. I've told you about the Energy from which all Arkanians are born and to which they return. It renews us in a special way called *Chehn-dürge*, a 'Life-storm' that nourishes our planet and keeps us alive. Now, you will see it for yourself, and it will be like nothing you have ever seen before."

The sky was electric purple, with clouds gathering into a huge, whirling funnel like a giant snake. Jeremy thought of Midwestern tornadoes, but this cloud was white, not dark, and much larger. The air was calm, but the funnel spun faster and faster, swelling at the top like the hood of a swaying cobra. Slowly, its color changed from the cotton-white of summer clouds to a deep, radiant gold. Sheet lightning flashed clear to the horizons, shimmering gold melting against the deep violet sky.

Bigger and bigger swelled the cobra's hood, filling up a third of the sky—and then from its opening mouth burst not venom but a drench of golden light that streamed in every direction, rippling as it fell to quench the land's thirst. The eyes of the Arkanians glowed in the radiant light-fall. Fur and feathers shimmered with color. Then *Chehn-dürge* faded, the sky was mild blue again, and everything was as before.

"Alright!" Jeremy murmured in an awe-struck tone. "That was the most beautiful thing I've ever seen!"

Alaikin's song began, stronger and sweeter than ever, as if refreshed by the golden storm. "We can live away from *Chehn-dürge*, but in time we weaken and must return to be renewed. Now, with the Energy fresh within us and our strength full, let's hurry to Earth, for the spite of *Ordúrrg-Zaikh* increases by the hour. Quick, Jeremy!"

9 WHERE'S THE MOUSE?

When Jeremy awoke, morning light was in his room and birds were chirping outside the window. He stretched lazily and opened one eye. Cleopatra was curled up by his side and the house was quiet. It was Sunday morning, so everybody was sleeping late. Jeremy had a nagging feeling that *he* was supposed to get up and do something, but he was too sleepy to remember what. Instead, he rolled onto his back and tried to recall his dreams. There'd been some sort of Space travel to weird planets with strange creatures. It had seemed so real, but now everything was faded and fuzzy. Why were the most exciting dreams the hardest to remember?

He was still in his pants and tee shirt, lying on top of the comforter with the edge pulled over for warmth. It wasn't even seven o'clock, so whatever he was supposed to do, there was plenty of time. He rolled onto his side to go back to sleep, but something was poking his leg. Digging his hand into his pocket, he felt the familiar shape of the ankh and pulled it out.

The stone was strangely warmer than it would have been from body heat. He opened an eye, looked at the ankh, and suddenly sat straight up, spilling Cleo off the bed and onto the rug. The black stone was cycling through a series of shimmering colors: red, orange, yellow, green, blue, purple, and then again. Was it vibrating in his hand, or was that his own pulse? He threw the comforter over his head, and in the darkness the ankh shone more brightly.

"The Flowering Crystal," Jeremy murmured, "*Zhystrém Haistrál,*" and everything came back to him at once. "Alaikin?" he whispered, searching the room. There was no answer, but a strand of melody wafted up from his memory, carrying with it words Alaikin had sung on Arkania.

"We cannot interfere with the worlds we guard . . . They must fight the battle themselves." Jeremy wanted to run away, just as he had on Arkania, but where could he go when nowhere was safe?

And what good would running do, he asked himself. None at all, came his own somber answer, except to let *Ordúrrg-Zaikh* win without even trying to stop it. Jeremy drew himself up straight, swung his legs over the edge of the bed, and planted them firmly on the floor. He might be destined to become Dragon food, but at least he had to try. The words of the Primal Tongue were becoming familiar to him now and came into his mind without effort. He was a *Ouyperkai*, a Guardian people depended on: Sara, Zack, everyone else. Jeremy felt himself begin to tremble, but he took a deep breath and tried to think of a plan.

Cleopatra jumped back onto the bed and rubbed against him, purring and nudging her head under his hand. He stroked her once and then held her head so he could look straight into her green-gold eyes. "What am I going to do, Cleo," he whispered. "I've got to find Grandpa's Book of Life, the *Shaiféir al Shehn*, and I don't even know where to start!"

Cleo stared back up at Jeremy and blinked solemnly. "Oh, you're a big help," he scolded. "All you want is to be petted. There *are* more important things, you know, and we've got to think fast."

"Well," Cleopatra answered, her voice purring pleasantly in Jeremy's mind, "when I'm tr-r-ying to catch a mouse, first I look for its hole."

"Cleo!" Jeremy gasped with astonishment, "You were mind-sharing with me! You never did that before."

"You never asked my opinion before. We cats are cr-r-reatures of few words, you know."

"It must have been Alaikin," Jeremy said. "He taught you how to do it."

"On the contr-r-rary," the cat responded, her voice meowy but clear in Jeremy's mind, like an telephone operator's in an old-time movie. "Alaikin taught *you* how to do it. I've always known."

She stretched, licked her paw, and groomed the hair on the back of her neck. "Would you mind scratching just behind this ear? There's a ter-r-rible itch."

Jeremy heard his mother's footsteps heading for the bathroom. "Mom would know what happened to Grandpa's stuff, wouldn't she?" he asked the cat, scratching her neck. "But I'll have to be careful not to make her suspicious."

"Pur-r-r?" Cleopatra said aloud, rubbing her head on Jeremy's wrist. The clear picture of Cleo's supper dish appeared in Jeremy's mind, and it certainly wasn't *his* thought. "How can you think about food at a time like this?" he scolded out loud.

"Pur-r-r?" said Cleo, and the evil odor of cat food welled up in his nostrils.

"Jeremy?" his mother called softly from the hall. "You're up early. Who are you talking to?"

"Oh, Mom," Jeremy said quickly, "I was just thinking out loud." To himself, he admitted that he still wasn't used to mind-sharing. Sometimes he talked out loud instead of *thinking* what he wanted to say.

"May I come in, Jerry?" his mother asked, opening the door to his room. Cleo jumped from the bed and was through the door in a flash. Jeremy smiled, knowing she was headed straight to her dish.

"Well," his mother said, smiling back, "up early and cheerful too. How nice, for a boy who's been so grumbly." She sat down on the edge of the bed.

"I'm sorry, Mom," Jeremy said. "It's just all the bad stuff that's been going on, with Gramps and Sara and all."

"Jerry," his mother replied softly, running her hand through his hair. "I wasn't trying to make you feel bad again. Yesterday, when you ran out of the kitchen, I was trying to tell you that even your father and I are irritable now. It's natural when people are upset."

Jeremy had slipped the ankh back into his pocket as his mother came into the room, and now he could feel it, warm and—yes—pulsing slightly in his grip. "I didn't really mean what I said yesterday," he told his mother, "about Sara not getting better. I think she will, really I do."

"I know you didn't mean it, Jerry. I've been thinking that you must be very lonely. We moved to this new neighborhood not long ago, and with all the attention we've had to give Sara, we haven't been able to spend time with you. Maybe you were angry with us, when you said that about her."

"No, Mom, I don't think so. It's just that things seemed kind of hopeless all of a sudden. Like nothing was ever going to change, and maybe it was my fault."

"Why would you think any of this is your fault?" his mother said wonderingly. "Sometimes bad things just happen, Jeremy. You can't hold yourself responsible when they have nothing to do with you. I know you're pretty sensitive, but don't blame yourself for everything that goes wrong!"

"Aw, Mom," Jeremy replied, glancing down at the floor and trying to look as if he believed her. What she didn't know was that he might have a really good reason for blaming himself— he just couldn't be sure. He thought of all the times his teasing went too far and ended only when Sara burst into tears. And then he remembered the sickening thud when the football hit her, how her head bounced off the sod when she fell, and how she seemed to take ages to stop her shuddering sobs. And how, with her face still shining wet, she sweetly promised she wouldn't tell anyone. She didn't want to get Jeremy in trouble, even though he deserved it. Sandy was right—Sara was a terrific kid. But Jeremy said nothing about any of this to his mother.

Cleopatra poked her nose into the room, licking her chops and yawning. She padded quickly over the carpet, jumped onto the bed, and pushed her head under Jeremy's mother's hand. "Eating, petting, and sleeping, that's all you care about," Jeremy thought. Cleo purred contentedly as his mother stroked her, and the cat looked at Jeremy with queenly disdain.

"Cats were sacred to the ancient Egyptians," Cleo thought proudly, "and when the Assyrian army attacked holding up cats as shields, the Egyptian archers wouldn't shoot their arrows. So my ancestors conquered Egypt. And what great things have you accomplished? We're still sitting here doing nothing, aren't we?"

Jeremy's mother watched her son and his cat stare at one another, laughing softly. "You and that cat," she said. "You talk to her and, honestly, sometimes I think she talks back."

"Oh no, Mom," Jeremy said quickly. "She never says anything. She just likes me, that's all."

Cleo flattened her ears against her head and looked at Jeremy with withering scorn, as if he were nothing but a fly.

"Mom," Jeremy said, ignoring the moody cat, "what happened to all of Grandpa's stuff? You know, his books and everything he brought back from Egypt?"

"Well," his mother said slowly, "he left most of the valuable things to the Museum. And then he gave a lot of the books to his friend Mr. MacIvery. You met him, didn't you? The old Scotsman who has that antique store over on Twelfth Street?"

"Gramps took me there a few times," Jeremy said, trying to hide his mounting excitement. "It's full of antique stuff from all over the world, masks and vases and lamps and things. And he's got this back room with books right up to the ceiling, the way Gramps's apartment used to be."

"Yes," Jeremy's mother said, "that's the place. Your father and I have a few things, like the sphinxes in the living room and the wall hangings, just to remember him by. Why do you ask, Jerry?"

"Oh, I don't really care," Jeremy said, shrugging his shoulders to seem more convincing. "I was just curious."

"Jerry," his mother said quietly, "you still miss your grandfather, don't you? It's not wrong to miss him, you know, and even to cry about it. I still do, sometimes. But I hope you're not as upset as your sister."

"No, Mom, come on! I'm not going to go looking for him in holes all over the place, if that's what you mean."

Jeremy's mother sighed and stroked his cheek. "That's good, Jeremy. I worry about you too, you know."

"Aw, Mom."

"Okay, let's talk about more cheerful things. Your father and I have decided that we should all go to the park for a picnic this afternoon. We've been moping around too much and it's time we had some fun. You can go out and play this morning, but be sure to be back by noon."

"Mom!" Jeremy lied, "I was going to do stuff with Zack and Sandy this afternoon."

"Well, they can come too if their father agrees. You ask him this morning. I'm sure he'd like a break from those two."

Jeremy's mother ran her hand over his wrinkled pants leg. "You've been sleeping in your clothes again," she said sternly.

"Geez, Mom, I only do it because it's more comfortable."

"Never mind, this time," she said, smiling. "But you *do* have a very comfortable pair of pajamas, and I want you to wear them to bed like any other boy. Tell you what, Jer, you wash up and change and I'll fix you some cereal and fruit. Be quiet, though. Sara and your father are still sleeping."

When Jeremy came back from the bathroom he found Cleo curled up in the middle of his bed, resting her chin on the bunched-up comforter. "Now what do you say, smarty-pants?" he whispered to her. "I've found out where the *Shai-féir al Shehn* is. All I have to do is get to Mr. MacIvery's shop."

Cleopatra batted her ears and yawned. "I *think*," she thought, "you've found the mouse-hole, but you're a long way from catching the mouse. As for what I *say*—mrrrowww!" And she jumped down and padded off to eat another breakfast.

10 SPECTERS AND SQUIRRELS

When Jeremy came out of his house, Zack was sitting on the front steps, waiting. Just my luck, Jeremy thought—the last person I wanted to see. Zack squinted in the sunlight, and Jeremy noticed a slight red glint in his eye.

"You're up early," Zack said with a forced grin. "Whatcha doing?"

"Nothing much," Jeremy said. "I've got to go somewhere. For a violin lesson."

"You forgot your violin, then," Zack snapped, the grin frozen on his face. "You gonna play on a comb?"

"Mine's broken," Jeremy lied quickly. "My teacher's going to let me use hers. You're up awful early yourself. Where's Sandy?"

"Still asleep. I got up early to wait for you. I know you're not going to any violin lesson."

"Oh yes I am," Jeremy said. "I'm going down to the corner to catch the bus to Twelfth Street. That's where my lesson is. What do you know about it anyway?"

"You forget I'm a genius, Jeremy," Zack said with a queer twitch of his lips. "I know all kinds of things. Like I know you don't have a music lesson on Sunday. You always go on Friday, after school."

"It's a special one," Jeremy said desperately. He didn't like lying any more than he liked fighting, and he knew he wasn't any good at either.

"Okay," Zack replied. "I'll go with you then. I kind of feel like a bus ride."

As they walked to the bus stop, the words of the Flowering Crystal echoed in Jeremy's mind. "You have seen the

Zaikhthréem go forth to infect the worlds," the *Zhystrém Haistrál* had said. "Beware, for now they will seek you."

Jeremy shuddered, and from the corner of his eye he saw the evil grin creep onto Zack's face again. "My God," Jeremy thought, "he knows. The *Zaikhthréem* know. Help me, Alaikin, the Spawn are coming!" But there was no answer.

"Hey, you guys!" Sandy yelled, running after them as they approached the bus stop, "wait up! Where are you going?"

"Jeremy says he's got a music lesson," Zack said, smirking. "And he wants me to come along for the ride. He doesn't want you."

"I do too," Jeremy said as Sandy came huffing up. "That is, I don't really want either of you, but Sandy gets to come if you do."

"Well," Sandy said to Jeremy, "I can go anyplace I want and it just so happens I want to go on the next bus. It's a free country, isn't it?"

"You can come, Sandy," Jeremy said. "I want you to. It's Zack who's being weird."

Zack grinned at Sandy and Jeremy and then turned and walked away. He stopped a few yards down the sidewalk, picked up a buckeye nut from somebody's lawn, and threw it at some crows on the telephone wire across the street. It was a typical Zack throw: the large nut missed by so much that the birds didn't even move. He picked up another nut and got ready to throw again.

"Jeremy," Sandy said in a low voice, "am I glad to see you! I've never seen Zack act like this before. I mean, he's always been kind of a fruitcake, but basically nice. Now it's like he's trying to be as mean as he can."

"I could maybe tell you why," Jeremy said, but then he stopped. She'd never believe him, and then she'd think he was crazier than Zack. It was the worst feeling in the world, to know something and not be able to tell it. This must be how Sara felt—she knew something was wrong but she was too sick to explain it. And so alone, completely alone.

"What's Zack been doing, anyway?" Jeremy asked.

"Well," Sandy began, "after he came out of his room for dinner last night he kept picking on me. He said nasty things, and when Dad made him stop he spilled a bowl of hot soup on me. He tried to make it look like an accident, but it wasn't.

"Dad made him say he was sorry, and for a minute I thought he really meant it. It was like he was going to start crying or something. Then Dad told him to go to his room and Charley followed him, like he always does. And then—I don't believe it, Jeremy—Zack kicked Charley! He loves Charley, but he kicked him, hard."

They watched Zack throw at the birds and stamp on the sidewalk when he missed. "There's something happening, Sandy," Jeremy said. "I can't tell you about it now but I know something strange is happening. Maybe I can tell you later."

"What is going on, Jeremy?" Sandy asked. "It's not just Zack, is it? I was watching this funny movie on TV last night and all of a sudden the channels started switching like crazy, and there was this weird program that wasn't supposed to be on. A horrible burned-up city, and people wandering around, hungry and crying. I went to tell Dad but he was on the computer. He said it was probably just static electricity and I should turn it off.

"It's so weird around here, Jeremy. I can't stand it. I wish we could go a thousand miles away."

Just as Jeremy was wondering why Sandy had said "we," Zack yelled "Hey, you guys, look what I found!"

"What is it?" Sandy and Jeremy asked, trotting over to where Zack stood beneath a buckeye tree.

He was pointing at a branch about half-way up. A gray squirrel crouched there, busily chewing as it turned a nut in its forepaws.

"How neat," Sandy said. "Look how he's got his tail curled over his back, right up to his head. It looks like a little crown. I bet he'll come down if we give him a nut." She bent down, picked up a buckeye nut, and held it out. "Here, squirrel," she called. "Here, little squirrel, come get this yummy nut!"

The squirrel froze, looked at Sandy for a second, and then went right on eating. "Don't be silly, Sandy," Zack said. "He's not going to come after *your* nut when he's already got one."

"Aw, but he's so cute," Sandy answered. "Maybe he'll come when he's done with that nut."

"We can make him come," Zack grinned. He picked up a stone from the sidewalk and handed it to Jeremy. "You've got the good arm, Jer. See if you can bean him. That'll get him down all right."

"Don't, Jeremy," Sandy said, "it's mean."

Jeremy weighed the stone in his hand, tossing it up and catching it a few times. He knew his arm was really good, and if he could get that squirrel, everybody would know just how good. Nobody would think he was a loser then. They'd think he was the greatest, and after all it was only a stupid squirrel.

"Jeremy-y-y!" Sandy moaned.

It was as if she were far away on a hill, not standing beside him. He looked at the squirrel, furry and bright on its branch, and the squirrel looked back. It seemed almost to be waiting for him, inviting him to throw. Suddenly, he felt icily calm and perfectly cruel, like a gun ready to go off. There was no Jeremy, no Sandy, no squirrel. There was nothing in the world but his brain rehearsing the throw, and the target.

Jeremy brought his arm back and aimed. He saw the squirrel as if through a gun sight—not with his naked eye. Someone else seemed to be moving his arm, someone else aiming. Laughter bubbled up inside him and tried to burst out. Vicious laughter that stung his throat.

"No, Jeremy!" Sandy shrieked, and this time he heard.

As his arm whipped forward, he recognized the laughter within: the same as in the Dragon's cave, the same as when Cleo was about to leap at Alaikin. At the last instant, he threw off his aim and missed the squirrel by a few inches. It dropped its nut and scampered further off on the branch.

81

"Jeremy," Sandy gasped, "you almost hit him."

He heard, but he didn't answer. He was listening to the voice of the *Zhystrém Haistrál* chiming in his memory. "Now you know the power of *Ordúrrg-Zaikh*. Fear and greed: these are its weapons."

"It's true," Jeremy murmured to himself. "For one second, I was afraid everybody would make fun of me if I didn't try to hit that squirrel, and greedy to prove I had the best arm in the world."

Sandy stared at Jeremy as if he'd gone crazy, but Zack smiled into his face as if he knew exactly what Jeremy meant. "That was just a lousy shot, Jer," Zack said, bending to pick up another stone. "I'll nail him, even though he's farther away now."

Zack threw with power and accuracy that were not his. Sandy shrieked as the stone hit the squirrel. The animal fell to the ground and lay there, stunned and bleeding from its ear, as she ran to help. When she reached down, it struggled to its feet and stumbled away. They heard it crawl slowly up the back side of the tree, out of sight.

"The bus is coming," Zack said calmly. His voice was cold and his face blank, but tears trickled down his cheeks.

In Jeremy's mind, the words of the *Zhystrém Haistrál* chimed again. "He is in grave danger, but the love that was in him is there still."

He remembered the day Zack and he had become blood brothers, swearing a sacred oath always to defend each other. On one of their explorations, Jeremy had fallen, stepping through a rotten piece of floorboard in an old, burnt-down house in an overgrown field. They'd named it the Haunted House because they'd met a kid nearby who told them that the old lady who lived there had burned to death in the fire and still showed up at night as a ghost surrounded by a halo of flames.

Zack had smiled down at him anxiously as he pulled him out with both hands, bracing against one of the remaining support posts, scorched but still standing. It was the opposite of their first meeting, when they'd crashed their bikes and Jeremy had pulled Zack to his feet. This time, as Jeremy reached out to keep himself from falling all the way through the floor, he caught his hand on a rusty nail. Typically, as soon as Jeremy was free, Zack began describing the horrors of tetanus in gruesome detail.

"Oh man, they call it lockjaw because your jaw locks up and you can't open your mouth and all you can do is drool and shake and then every muscle in your body clenches, like when you're fierce cold, and that's called tetany. You won't be able to eat for a month and they'll have to feed you intravenously, that's through your veins with a needle, with this mixture of sugar and protein. Man, it's really bad."

And Jeremy had answered dryly, for once knowing as much as his friend, "Yeh, I've heard about tetanus, Zack—Dad keeps my booster up to date. So you won't get to see me jam up like a rusty padlock, sorry." Jeremy remembered grinning at Zack and then sucking the blood off the wound.

"Shoot," Zack had said. "That would have been cool. But you know what, I had my shot too, so now we can be blood brothers without catching lockjaw from each other. Check this out." Zack showed Jeremy a bloody scratch on his wrist from a floorboard splinter, and they squeezed their wounds and rubbed them together, mixing their blood. Then they clasped hands with their forearms pressed together.

"Now we have to fight for each other if either one of us is attacked, for the rest of our lives," Zack said.

Jeremy nodded and said "Amen."

"Do you think it was the old lady's ghost that led me onto that rotten board and made me break through?" Jeremy asked.

"Ghosts are insubstantial, just apparitions, like all specters, Zack replied. "They're not made out of real matter, so how could they act on anything substantial? And you are pretty damned substantial, Jeremy."

As Zack then explained all the words he'd used just to describe "ghosts," Jeremy had realized that what his friend wanted more than anything was to communicate. He was lonely with all of his knowledge and he wanted to share it, to teach it to someone else so he wouldn't be so alone. Telling his friends what he knew and having them understand and appreciate it meant more to Zack than anything else.

Now, with Zack moved to tears by injuring the squirrel, Jeremy thought that he might connect with him by doing what Zack himself would have done in better times—explain what was going on. He'd teach Zack about the Dragon, Spider, Sara, and the cosmic battle in which they had become involved. Maybe, vulnerable as he was in this moment, Zack would get it, and his brilliant mind could recapture his emotions and restore him to himself again.

Jeremy held out his right hand toward Zack, the same hand with which he'd clasped Zack's in their eternal blood bond. "Hey, check this out," he said in a tentative voice, planning to tell Zack all about *Ordúrrg-Zaikh* and the *Ouyperkain*.

But at that moment the bus, which had slowly been working its way up the street, picking up and letting off passengers, finally approached their stop. Zack wiped his face with his sleeve, clenched his jaw, and looked away as the Number 10 pulled up. Its doors whooshed open and the three friends filed up the front stairs in silence.

11 A BAD BIRD

For a while, Zack seemed almost his old self as the bus trundled downtown. He gabbed happily about his plans for Tyranno-man, all the while making paper airplanes from their transfers. "If I can just get the arms to stay on," he said excitedly, "it will be finished in time for Dad's birthday." He seemed to have forgotten about the squirrel completely, and Jeremy dared to hope that somehow *Ordúrrg-Zaikh* had lost its grip on him.

Zack and Jeremy tested the planes by flying them to and fro across the back seat, until the driver spotted them in his rear-view mirror. "You kids back there," the man said, "you better cool it. Just 'cause this bus is empty don't mean it's a playground."

Sandy had been brooding about the squirrel, but now she perked up and yelled back at the driver. "Sorry, Mister, but we've got this mad scientist back here and he's working on a supersonic fighter plane."

"Sure," the man said. "And my daddy's the President. I get time and a half on Sunday, but that don't mean I got to put up with rowdy kids."

"Don't worry Mister," Jeremy replied. "There's this special drug we give him when he gets too weird. Calms him right down."

"Well," the driver said, chuckling, "I guess I could use some of that. Where you kids gettin' off at?"

"Downtown, on Twelfth Street," Jeremy said.

"Yeah? And what are you gonna do down there?"

"Well," Jeremy said, and then he stopped. If only there were other passengers, so the driver wouldn't be so nosy. But there was nobody, and he had to tell Zack and Sandy something. It was no use sticking to the music lesson story.

"Well," he began again, "I had a music lesson but that got cancelled. So I'm going to Mr. MacIvery's antique store to find a present for my mom. She really loves antiques."

"Can't just go to Wal-Mart, huh?" the driver said, laughing. "They got some good antiques down there. Made in China, way back last week!"

"Ha, ha, ha!" Sandy whispered to Jeremy, "he's about as funny as a doorknob. But how do you know your lesson got cancelled when you aren't even there yet?"

"Jeremy's just no good at lying," Zack said quietly, the red glint returning to his eyes. "Maybe he'll tell you what he's up to, Sandy, because he sure won't tell me."

As he realized that the *Zaikthréem* still controlled Zack, Jeremy's heart sank. "Aw," he said to Sandy, pausing while his mind fumbled for the best story, "I just made it up about the lesson. I was really always going to get something for Mom. Mr. MacIvery was Gramps's friend, and he's got lots of cool stuff. I wanted to keep it a secret and surprise Mom."

"Well, we can keep a secret," Sandy said. "Maybe we can help you pick out something."

"That's not the real secret," Zack snickered. "His mom's birthday isn't till February, and it's kind of early for Christmas. Jeremy's not telling the real secret."

"You're wrong, Zack," Jeremy said, "you can give somebody a present just because you want to—not only on their birthday or at Christmas. Mom's been so down about Sara lately that I wanted to give her something nice to cheer her up."

It wasn't true, or at least not until that very moment when he'd conveniently thought it up, Jeremy reflected guiltily, but at least it had shut up Zack. All he could do was snort and settle into a wicked scowl.

"Jeremy, that's so sweet," Sandy said, and Jeremy felt the screw of guilt turn deeper in his guts.

Man, he thought, I really hate lying—even for a good reason—and it's almost worse when I pull it off. It ate at him that in making up a story for Zack, without meaning to, he'd also conned Sandy into thinking better of him than he deserved. She was the last person he wanted to weasel into liking him based on a lie.

"Twelfth Street," the driver called out. "Antique shop, bums, winos, junkies, and old alley cats. You kids be careful down here, and don't talk to strangers. This ain't no family-type area, and real bad stuff can happen. You hear what I'm sayin'?"

Sandy stuck out her tongue at the man as they trooped out the back door. The bus whooshed away like a boat rushing off to sea and left them stranded on the sidewalk.

Bright sunshine glittered off broken glass that littered the curb, and the sharp glare was scarily blinding. Jeremy squinted uncertainly up and down the block trying to locate Mr. MacIvery's sign. "I hope I can find it," he said. "It was two years ago when I was here with Gramps."

"Try over there," Zack said, pointing at a small black sign with old-style lettering in the next block.

"How do you know?" Jeremy asked. "You've never been there, have you?"

"I just know," Zack said smugly.

"This is a really rotten neighborhood," Sandy said. "There's a drunk back in that alley over there. Or maybe he's on drugs. I wish we had Charley with us."

"That guy won't bother us," Jeremy said, trying to sound sure of himself. "And Charley's half blind anyway. Zack's right though, Sandy. The shop's over there—I remember now."

"Hey," the drunk called, "you kids! Come here, I got something to show ya's." They broke into a run at the alley and kept on running past a broken-down car inside of which somebody slept on a pile of rags. The shop wasn't far, but to Jeremy it seemed as if they were going in slow motion. An overflowing dumpster loomed near the corner, and then at last they stood, panting, in front of the run-down brick building. "MacIvery—Antiquities, Books, and Magic," read the rusty sign in its wrought-iron frame.

As Jeremy pushed through the door, a hand-bell tied to the inner knob tinkled. His shoes made a hollow thud on the wooden floor. The dim, dusty shop smelled like an old attic. A worn wooden Indian at the door guarded a crazy jumble of strange objects jamming the front room.

On both sides, chest-high stacks of oriental rugs were strewn with exotic stuffed animals and birds, embroidered pillows, old army helmets and canteens, and a few tarnished bugles and bayonets. In the middle were dressers, marble-topped end-tables, sewing machines with foot-pedals, grandfather clocks, old phonographs, fancy hat-racks, merry-go-round animals, intricate wicker bird cages, and an old-fashioned dress dummy topped with a huge plumed hat.

On top of anything with a flat top rose another hodge-podge: brass lamps and statues of wise chinamen, antique bottles, shrunken heads, old duck decoys, and bizarre, fish-looking things with huge goggle-eyes that might once have been alive but now were sealed in large, clear jars of oily liquid.

All around the walls were masks. Some were large and fierce, with horns and bright paint, and others small, with twisted, laughing mouths. The masks stared down at him through dark, empty eye-sockets.

Zack immediately started to examine the weird fish creatures in the jars. His coke-bottle eyeglasses reflected them as huge, twisted monsters. All was quiet. There seemed to be nobody in the shop.

"Hello!" Jeremy called down the narrow aisle to the back room. "Mr. MacIvery? Are you there?"

"Hello! How are you?" a voice screamed from the far corner of the room. Jeremy gasped with excitement. Was it the *baibaidínn*? Then he peered more carefully into the dim corner and saw a large green and red macaw tethered to its perch. "I'm fine, how are you?" the bird's hoarse voice answered itself. Not a *baibaidínn*, Jeremy thought in disappointment. At least, not *my baibaidínn*.

A chair creaked in the back room, footsteps scuffed along the aisle, and the bent figure of Mr. MacIvery appeared. He was an old man, older, or at least more wrinkled, than Grandpa Heinrich had been. But the eyes that peered over his reading glasses were sharp, and the hand that grasped Jeremy's was strong and steady.

"Can this be little Jeremy?" Mr. MacIvery mused. "Why, look how you've grown, in only a year—isn't it?"

"More like two years, Mr. MacIvery," Jeremy said, squirming in the old man's grip. "I'll be twelve and a half in two months."

"Twelve and a half, oh my goodness," Mr. MacIvery replied, chuckling and letting go of Jeremy's hand. "And you've brought friends, I see."

"These are Sandy and Zack. They're brother and sister, and they came to help me find a present for my mom."

"For your mother, oh yes, a very kind thing to give a present to your mother. I am pleased to meet you, Sandy and Zack, very pleased. Imagine, coming all the way down here on your own. Very ambitious, oh my."

Mr. MacIvery's voice sounded as rusty as his signpost, as if both had been hanging out in the rain for years. He stroked his stringy, yellow-gray beard and rubbed a bony index finger across his long, bumpy nose. There was a sort of narrow ledge halfway down this nose, and it seemed to Jeremy as if he must have grown it specially to keep his glasses from slipping.

The old man chuckled again and cleared his throat. "Yes, laddie, you might well examine this nose of mine. It's home-grown Scots, and it hasn't shrunk over the years like the rest of me. Keeps the specs in place, that it does."

"I'm sorry," Jeremy stammered, wishing he were more clever at disguising his feelings. It was yet another failing he could add to the list. "I didn't mean to stare."

"Of course you did," Mr. MacIvery said with a smile, "and quite rightly too." He peered over at Zack, who was still fascinated by the bottled fish-things.

"Well," Mr. MacIvery continued, "those beasties Zack is so fond of would not make a good present for one's mother, would they? They came from a carnival I once had a little to do with. *Mysteries of the Deep Blue Sea*, you know. Stuff and nonsense, yes? Mostly lamprey eels and baby sharks, I suspect. A present for one's mother, now. . . let me think what that might be."

Mr. MacIvery crossed the room with the springy stride of a much younger man, as if having a job to do—find the perfect gift and sell it to Jeremy—had given him new energy. On a pile of carpets lay a large stuffed crocodile. He reached behind the creature and squeezed its back left leg. Suddenly, the crock came alive, crawling toward Jeremy and his friends, mouth gaping and eyes flashing. Sandy shrieked and jumped back, dumping herself into a big old rocking chair that tilted so violently back and forth it almost spilled her out again.

"Never fear, lass," Mr. MacIvery chuckled, "I'll save you." He squeezed the animal's leg again. The big reptile creaked to a stop, frozen in a lunging posture, its jaws spread for a meal it would never catch. The rocker settled down as Sandy started to giggle and shoved her fist into her mouth. That was her trick to stifle herself before she was giggled breathless.

"I don't suppose your mother would approve of that, eh, Jeremy?" said the old man. "Something to keep prowlers from the door?"

"No, Mr. MacIvery," Jeremy said, sounding a bit disappointed. "I don't think so."

"Quite right, lad. Though I'll bet *you* would fancy it, or your friend over there, with the specs."

"Electric," Zack sneered. "It's nothing but a big electric toy. Haven't you got any real magic in this shop? Or is it all fake junk to impress kids, Mr. MacPhoney?"

"Zack!" Sandy said in a shocked voice, "why are you being such a jerk? I'm sorry, Mr. MacIvery, my brother's having a bad day."

The old man peered sharply over his glasses and Zack stared back with a smirk. "Got a live one here, haven't we?" Mr. MacIvery said, straightening up and taking a step toward Zack, looking as if he could put him down on the floor if he chose to. "So it's real magic you want, eh? Well, let me tell you, real magic is for those who won't take any harm from it or make any harm with it. And I'm not at all certain you're that type."

For a moment, Zack looked frightened, as if the shopkeeper were reading his mind. Then the smirk recaptured his face and he turned his back on Mr. MacIvery. "I don't care anyway," Zack yelled over his shoulder, as he wandered over to the macaw's corner.

"Hello," the bird said. "Good bird. Are you a good bird?"

"Might be a *bad* bird, that boy," Mr. MacIvery muttered, and Jeremy saw Zack stiffen.

12 MORE THAN ONE SURPRISE

"Let me see," the old man said, scratching his chin and peering around the shop. "A present for Jeremy's mother, is it?" He reached up and pulled down a mask from the wall, the face of a Chinese dragon with flames springing from its nostrils and a huge, red, curled-up tongue.

"This might keep her up at night," he said, putting on the mask, "but she could have some fun on Halloween." He pulled a leather cord on the side of the mask. The red eyeballs twirled in their sockets and the big tongue uncurled with a hiss.

"It sure would be nice if every dragon was a toy," Jeremy said, before he could stop himself.

"What's that you say?" Mr. MacIvery said intensely, taking off the mask and examining Jeremy closely. "What might you know about dragons? More than most lads your age, I can see that in your eyes. The eyes tell everything—you know that, don't you?"

Mr. MacIvery captured Jeremy's eyes with a glance as sharp as a needle. Jeremy winced, but held the old man's gaze, even though he badly wanted to look away.

"Your friend has honest, open eyes, lass," Mr. MacIvery said, turning to Sandy. "Can't even hide what he wants to. Brother Zack would do well to take a lesson from him. But I've no mind to meddle. Let Zack have his secrets, and much good may they do him."

Sandy gave Jeremy a puzzled look, but at that moment a loud ruckus of flapping wings and macaw screams came from the corner of the shop.

"It tried to bite me," Zack yelled. "Your damned bird tried to bite me."

"Ah well," Mr. MacIvery said mildly. "And what did you do to him?"

"I was only going to pet him," Zack said, "and, well, I wanted that loose feather in his tail."

"Then, you're very lucky he likes you. Because if he didn't, he wouldn't have tried to bite you. He would have *succeeded*, and a rough time you'd have had. Perhaps we'd better find something to keep you out of mischief. You're a danger to yourself, that you are. It's magic you want? Well then, magic you'll get."

Mr. MacIvery stepped behind the counter at the back of the room and pulled two small stone vials from a drawer. He uncorked them, spooned yellow powder from one and blue from the other into an old stoneware crock, smoke-blackened and chipped on one side, and mixed the powders together. Next, from a tiny leather-covered flask, he shook a few drops of clear liquid onto the mound. Last, he took a box of wooden kitchen matches from the drawer, lit one with a flourish, touched it to the mixture, and stepped back.

The three friends ducked back too, expecting a huge flash or an explosion, but nothing at all happened.

"Great magic you've got," Zack sneered at the old man. "It's just a bunch of dust."

"Well, he tried, didn't he?" Sandy snapped at her brother. "You don't have to be so rotten about it. It's not like all of your experiments work either."

Score one for Sandy, Jeremy thought happily as he grinned at her. They watched the old man smile, fold his arms, and wait, as if Zack hadn't bothered him at all, but Jeremy felt he had to say something about it. "I'm really sorry Zack's not behaving, Mr. MacIvery," he said, disgusted with his friend's nastiness, "but like Sandy said, he's not feeling well today."

Mr. MacIvery nodded to Jeremy and then swept out his right arm, palm up, in the direction of the worn, dark crock.

Slowly, a rainbow took shape above the powder, shimmering out to the ends of the counter.

"Look!" Jeremy whispered to the squabbling brother and sister, half holding his breath for fear of spoiling it. In the violet space beneath the rainbow, a golden mist gathered and sifted down, a mist that meant something very special to someone who had witnessed the Arkanian *Chehn-dürge*.

"Alright!" Zack shouted, startling everyone. "You did it, Mr. MacIvery!"

For a moment, Zack was his old goofy self, wild to learn or experience anything new, so happy and excited that he jumped up and down. But as the golden mist faded, so did his smile, leaving his face once again sullen. It was as if he had opened a beautifully wrapped Christmas present and found nothing inside.

"You ought to make him give you that for your mother, Jeremy," Zack sneered. "I bet it kills bugs or something."

"Zack!" Sandy snapped, "You are such a creep! That was the most beautiful thing I've ever seen!"

"Don't fret, lass," Mr. MacIvery said. "Your brother's not quite himself, but he'll come right again. Just give him time."

"Could we have some of that powder?" Jeremy asked timidly. "For sure Mom would like that."

"I'm sorry, Jeremy, but no," the old man said firmly. "You see, these powders take the form of the wishes and dreams of whoever uses them. In the wrong hands they would be entirely unpredictable. Who knows what nightmares might get loose. The powders are only for show, not for sale."

"That's too bad, Mr. MacIvery," Jeremy said sadly. "They're really neat. But what about a book, then? My mom's a teacher, so she really likes books."

"Oh, well, if it's a book you want, just come with me to the back room," the old Scotsman replied. "You'll find books aplenty, oh my, yes."

Jeremy and Sandy followed him into the back room of the store, but Zack skulked behind, staring at the ashes that remained in the crock. Just as Jeremy remembered, books lined the walls right up to the ceiling. For a while, he scanned the rows, searching for dark leather with golden designs. But there were so many books that he soon gave up and stared glumly at the floor.

"Is it a particular book you want then, lad?" Mr. MacIvery asked pointedly, as Zack came into the room.

"Yes," Jeremy answered hopefully. "It's a big leather book with golden pictures all over the cover. It used to be my grandpa's, but Mom told me he gave it to you."

"Oh, that book," the old man said slowly, as if counting every word. "You wouldn't be wanting that book for your mother, *would* you? That book has other purposes—and your friend here seems very interested in it too."

Jeremy turned, and Zack's eyes bored into his with such intensity, almost glowing red, that he had to turn away again.

"Where is that book, Mr. MacIvery?" Zack asked through clenched teeth. "That's the book we want!"

"I'm sorry to disappoint you both," the shopkeeper said pleasantly, "but that particular book is where it should be, safe in the Museum."

"The Museum!" Jeremy exclaimed gloomily. "I guess I'll never get that one, then."

"You needn't look so miserable," the old Scotsman replied. "There are plenty of other books. Here's *A Mother's Handbook*," he said, pulling out a thin, worn volume that must have been at least a hundred years old. "Everything she'll ever need to know to raise you up right," he said with a grin, "at least in Nineteenth Century St. Louis. And here's *The Animals Run the Circus*, with pictures too," he continued, opening a gray book with a scuffed cover to show a picture of a tiger with a whip in its teeth coaxing a cowering animal trainer to jump through a flaming hoop.

"Plenty of books here, Jeremy, just choose one."

"That's okay, Mr. MacIvery," Jeremy replied in a sinking voice. "I really only wanted that one." He felt doubly bad because he hadn't gotten anything for his mother, which seemed like a good idea now even though he hadn't even thought of it before he'd had to, *and* he had let down Mr. MacIvery, who was pursing his lips trying to hide the disappointment of losing a sale.

"Well then, I expect you'll need to be going," the old man said, gazing off a little wistfully at the ceiling. "Time is pressing, eh?" He scratched his chin and caught Jeremy's eye. "That is, if you truly need that book and none other."

"You can always find a present later, Jeremy," Sandy said cheerfully. "After all, it isn't even near Christmas yet."

As Mr. MacIvery led them toward the door, Jeremy glanced around a little desperately, trying to find something to buy in order to cheer up both the old Scotsman and his mom. A small, wooden mask of a serenely smiling woman's face caught his eye. Smooth and oval-shaped, it was painted white with red lips and golden highlights, and Jeremy felt calmer the moment he saw it, even in his anxious state.

"What about that mask, Mr. MacIvery," he blurted, pointing at it, "I think it might make Mom feel really peaceful."

The shopkeeper brightened and stretched to get down the mask. "You have good taste, Jeremy. This is a Ko-mote mask, used in Japanese Noh theatre. Noh plays are very formal, and only men can act in them, so they need masks to play women. This one is of a beautiful young woman, a calm and contented spirit. It's nicely done, but it is a replica, so I can let you have it for far less than an original—let's say, twelve dollars. I'll wrap it up for you. Your mother should be very pleased!"

A few minutes later the friends were out on the street, Jeremy carefully holding the bagged mask. The sky was clouding up as if a storm was moving in, and the air clung clammily to their skin. As they walked silently back toward the bus stop, Sandy kicked a stone along the sidewalk. They forgot all about the drunk until he darted from the alley, grabbed Jeremy's arm, and pulled him into the street.

96

"Watch out, Jeremy," Sandy yelled, grabbing his other arm and pulling against the man's grip. "Zack!" she screamed at her brother, "don't just stand there. Help me!"

It happened so fast that Jeremy was more startled than afraid. He clutched his package tightly, thinking the man was trying to rob him, but the drunk's pull was too weak to budge his arm—as if all he wanted was to hold Jeremy's attention.

"Can you see them," the man whispered hoarsely as Jeremy looked up into his eyes. "I see them all the time. Red crawly things. Get 'em out, can't you? Help me get 'em out!"

At that moment, the bus came roaring down the street. Half a block away, the driver saw them, hit his horn, and held it. The drunk lost his grip, and Jeremy nearly fell on Sandy, who still tugged on his other arm. The man staggered away, whimpering and rubbing his eyes. Zack stood and stared as if he recognized him. Sandy grabbed her brother with her free hand and dragged both him and Jeremy toward the bus.

"Looks like you had a little excitement there," the driver said as he pulled away. "I warned you 'bout this neighborhood, didn't I?"

"Just an old wino," Zack said scornfully. "He was so drunk he couldn't have hurt a fly."

"Ain't you the brave one," the driver said, clicking his tongue. "You're lucky I scared him off and you ain't hurt none."

As the driver shook his head, Jeremy sighed and leaned back into his seat. Staring out the window, trembling just slightly, he felt Sandy's hand on his shoulder.

"Are you okay, Jeremy?" she said softly.

"Yeah," he answered, squirming a little beneath her grip. "I'm alright. He wasn't trying to hurt me. He just thought I could help him."

"What?" Sandy blurted. "No way could you help somebody like him!"

"I know," Jeremy replied. "I only wish I could."

13 THREE CAN PLAY AT THIS

When Jeremy got home, he hid the mask under his shirt, smuggled it into his room, and put it under some sweaters on the top shelf of his closet. He wanted to surprise his mom with it when things calmed down. Now, she was running around the house gathering everything for the picnic.

"It's nothing fancy, Mr. Tatum," she said to Zack and Sandy's father on the phone. "Just a hotdog roast, and the kids can wander around the trails. We'll be back around three."

Three o'clock, Jeremy thought to himself. The Museum was only open till five! "Mom," he asked, interrupting the phone call, "are we really going to be back by three?"

"Jeremy, *I'm on the phone*," his mother said, covering the mouthpiece and hammering each word in exasperation. "What does it matter when we get back? Forgive me, Mr. Tatum, that was just Jeremy being rude. What did you say?"

"Sorry, Mom," Jeremy whispered, hanging his head but tapping his foot in frustration. There was a 3:30 bus that should get him to the Museum a little after four. That would leave only thirty minutes after they got back to lose Zack somehow—but how? And then he'd have less than an hour at the Museum to find the *Shaiféir al Shehn*!

Standing beside his mother, Jeremy heard Mr. Tatum's tired voice rasp over the line. "It's very kind of you to take them, Mrs. Taylor. I'd go myself, but my computer went down last week and I've got to make up the time."

"Geez," Jeremy said after his mother hung up. "I wish he could come. Sandy says all he does is work."

"You know, Jerry," his mother said, "Mr. Tatum has to support Sandy and Zack all by himself, on just one salary, and take care of the mortgage too. Even two parents have all they can do to make a living for their family, and for a single parent it's really tough."

"But kids have problems too," Jeremy muttered as started for his bedroom. "Boy, do they ever!"

Cleopatra lay curled up on the bed across Jeremy's jacket, basking in a sunbeam. "Meow," she said lazily, purring as he came into the room.

"Meow yourself," Jeremy replied grumpily.

Suddenly, Cleo's purring was inside Jeremy's head, and then the burr of her voice, so loud he nearly jumped. "My, we *are* cr-r-abby," she thought. "You humans should sleep more. It's so r-r-relaxing." She stretched from head to foot and dug her claws deliciously into his jacket.

"Cleo," Jeremy said, "you scared me. I almost forgot you could mind-share." He walked over to the bed and began to pet her. The cat wriggled with pleasure. "There's no time to tell you what happened, Cleo, but Mr. MacIvery doesn't have *The Book of Life.*"

"I know," Cleo's voice purred happily. "The *Shaiféir-r-r al Shehn* is in the Museum, and you have to go on a picnic."

"You knew where it was all the time!" Jeremy thought angrily. "And I just wasted the whole morning at the antique shop because you didn't tell me."

"Silly boy," she purred on, "of course I didn't know. But I do *now*. It's all in your mind, plain as my whiskers. Scratch my tummy, there. R-r-right."

"Cleo," Jeremy thought, "Zack's much worse now. Even Mr. MacIvery noticed. I'm afraid the Spawn are spreading."

"Mr. MacIvery tried to help you," the cat purred, "but he couldn't get around Zack. The *Zaikhthréem* have too firm a grip on him—I can see that from your memories." Cleo sat up, licked her paw, and started washing herself all over.

"Then Mr. MacIvery knows?" Jeremy asked. "I thought he said some pretty strange things. Could he be a Guardian? Alaikin said there were more of them, but then he said Grandpa was the last great one of his generation."

"Per-r-haps," thought the cat, "Mr. MacIvery only became a *Ouyper-r-rkai* after your grandfather died."

"Jerry!" his father yelled from the driveway, "come out here and help me get this grill into the car, will you please?"

"You'd better get going," Cleo purred.

"And what will you do," Jeremy teased, "sleep all day while I handle the hard stuff?"

"What a mar-r-velous idea," Cleo purred. She patted down Jeremy's jacket, wrapped herself in her tail, and curled up.

"Queen Cleopatra," Jeremy muttered. "Empress of the Nile. All she did was lounge on her barge, just like you on my bed."

"Oh no, she did much more than that, like rule an empire, but you're right, she did know how to live." Cleo yawned.

"Jeremy!" his father shouted again.

* * *

Russell Park was about thirty miles down the highway. It wasn't much more than a few barbecue pits, two asphalt tennis courts, and a volleyball court, behind which a mile or so of forest trail wound back and forth across a creek. Jeremy knew the place because his Dad had taken him there to practice tennis, and after playing they'd hiked around to cool down. That was when they still did fun things.

In the picnic area, they were the only party, so they had plenty of room to play touch football and Frisbee while the barbecue got set up. Jeremy's mother laughed when his father, who didn't believe in starter fluid, couldn't keep the fire going.

"Why should it be any different this time?" she teased him, while he alternated between pressing his lips together with embarrassment or impatience and pursing them to blow on the charcoal and help the fire take hold. At last the coals turned white, the hotdogs were roasted and scarfed down, the potato salad eaten, and the fruit salad ignored because everyone had filled up on everything else.

Jeremy's mother settled down with a paperback novel and his father began to play out a chess game from the newspaper. For a moment, Jeremy thought of challenging his father to a game of chess, to at least delay the coming confrontation with Zack that already had his stomach in knots. From Zack, he'd learned more opening gambits and now played a pretty good game. But his dad was far better, and Jeremy could never beat him.

Dr. Taylor didn't believe in letting Jeremy win at chess, he told his son, and he felt the same way about tennis, or anything else. Jeremy hadn't gotten anywhere arguing about this.

"You don't learn that way," his father said. "Even if you keep losing, you want to learn something from your opponent each time, so one day you'll win. And you'll get tougher only if you fight the odds, not if you get a cheap break."

Jeremy wasn't sure he agreed—just once in a while he'd like to win, even if he knew his father had let him. His mom took his side, insisting that it wouldn't hurt if he were allowed to win, and might even build up his confidence.

"Just because you worked with the Marines," he had overheard her telling his dad one night when they thought he was asleep, "doesn't mean you have to act like one, and Jeremy doesn't either. The tough get going and all that, okay, but Jerry's just a kid. I think you need to cut him some slack now and then."

"No, Laurie," his dad responded, "he's got to earn it. I love Jeremy as much as you, but I don't believe I'd be doing him any favors if I let him win. He'd end up a loser, always thinking somebody will hand him the solution whenever he has trouble—and they won't."

Yet even though he never won a chess or a tennis match against his dad, Jeremy sometimes took pieces, made tennis shots, and even won a few tennis games that he shouldn't have, when his dad seemed to let up a bit. He smiled to himself. Maybe Dad secretly had a soft side but wanted nobody to know that he didn't completely follow his own macho code. So he let his kid win points, but never a match.

Anyway, Jeremy concluded, only two people could play chess, they hadn't brought their tennis racquets, and he had to find a way to get Sandy away from Zack. Playing a game wouldn't do that. But he also had to avoid a fight with Zack, which could happen if they were away from his parents. That possibility scared him stiff. Maybe even harder, given Sandy's worry about her brother, would be to persuade her to ditch him for a while.

Slowly, a plan came together in Jeremy's mind. The big attraction at the park was an area where the creek cut through a deep gorge, surrounded on both sides by high rock walls. That was where he needed to take them.

"Mom, Dad," Jeremy said, "I'm going to show Sandy and Zack the trails—they've never seen them before."

"Okay, Jerry," his father answered, "but if you see any wild animals, stay away from them. One or two cases of rabid animal bite were reported in this area last month, so I want you to be extra careful."

"Don't worry, Dad," Jeremy said. "We'll watch out. Come on, you guys."

At first, Jeremy walked through the woods, but when they came to the steep slope down into the gorge, he grabbed Sandy's hand and took off running.

"Catch us if you can!" he shouted over his shoulder. Sandy and he were much faster than Zack, who ran as if fighting a stiff wind, and when they reached a branch in the trail he was out of sight. One path went up and over the rock wall, and the other continued along the stream.

"Hey, you guys, wait up!" Zack called from far back on the trail.

"We'd better wait for him," Sandy said. "He might get lost."

"No, come on, Sandy," Jeremy panted, "I've got to talk to you. Zack won't get lost—the trail loops around."

Jeremy took off his cap, threw it on the upward path, and then towed Sandy down toward the creek until they came to a cave under the cliff. It was about the size of the living room in Jeremy's house, and a huge rock jutted at an angle from the back wall. Jeremy pulled Sandy into the pocket behind the rock. He put his finger to his lips and crouched down, pulling her with him.

They heard Zack pounding up to the fork in the trail, where he stopped and scuffed around. "Hey," he called out, "it's not funny anymore. Come on, which way did you guys go?"

Sandy started to get up, but Jeremy grabbed her arm. "He'll be okay," he whispered, "honest. Come on, Sandy, stay here. You want to help him, don't you?"

Zack's voice came faintly through the rock wall. "Oh yeah, Jeremy. Real smart trick with the hat. Forgot about your footprints though, didn't you?"

Zack's footfalls slowly approached as Jeremy kicked himself inwardly for yet another dumb move. Too much was at stake, he thought tensely, for him to screw up again.

"You've got to go for it," his father had told him fifty times. "Tell yourself that failure is not an option. And if you screw up, you figure out why and fix it, and next time you go for it again."

It's easy enough for you to say, Dad, Jeremy answered in the tense silence between his thoughts. You never even screw up the first time—and I'll bet you've never had so much at risk!

If I don't get it together, Jeremy brooded, even Alaikin might have nothing more to do with me, and find another *Ouyperkai* after all. He almost wished for that, but the very thought of it stung him to the marrow. He'd be so ashamed of himself he'd have to crawl behind the couch and never come out. No, scary as things are, Jeremy thought, I've got no good choice *but* to go for it.

Holding Sandy's arm, he shrank back into the cool shadows. "Shhhh!" he whispered to her. Zack appeared in the dazzle of sunlight at the mouth of the cave. Everything was quiet except for the rippling of the creek and the harsh cawing of a crow, a noise like a rusty iron door slowly closing.

"I found you," Zack called uncertainly, peering into the cave. "Come on, get out of there!" He stepped into the cave and then stopped. "I can't see a thing," he said, "my glasses are all fogged up with sweat."

In the silence, Jeremy imagined him taking off his glasses and rubbing them on his shirt.

"Come on, you guys," Zack pleaded. "You know I can hardly see in the dark."

Sandy moved and Jeremy tightened his grip on her arm and laid his other hand gently across her lips. A few seconds passed.

"I don't see them," Zack muttered to himself. "Maybe they went on." His footsteps echoed in the cave as he turned and plodded heavily down the path.

"Okay," Sandy said quietly, jerking her mouth free of Jeremy's hand and wriggling her arm out of his grip. "What is this all about?"

"Sandy," Jeremy said, "when we get back home, would you do me a favor?"

"What?" she answered.

"I've got to get away from Zack," Jeremy continued. "He's been following me all day. Can you keep him busy for half an hour, just until I catch the downtown bus?"

"Why?" Sandy asked, looking puzzled. "You're supposed to be Zack's friend."

"If I told you, you wouldn't believe me."

"Try me."

Jeremy opened his mouth, but nothing came out. How could he tell her about the *Zhystrém Haistrál*, Alaikin,

Ordúrrg-Zaikh and the insidious *Zaikhthréem?* It was just too mind-blowing. She'd think he was messing with her or completely wacko, and even if he could persuade her it would take way too long. Time was something he did not have. It was hard, being *Ouyperkai Orthein,* and he wasn't even doing it very well. It was the toughest thing he'd ever done.

"You know the book I was looking for at Mr. MacIvery's?" Jeremy began. "Remember, he said it was at the Museum? Well, I've got to get there and find it before they close."

"What for?" Sandy asked. "What good is an old book?"

"Sandy," Jeremy sighed, "it's too complicated to explain everything. You know how Sara is sick and Zack has been acting so crazy? Well, if I get this book, it could help them. But if Zack gets it, he could hurt himself—or somebody else."

"What?" Sandy exclaimed. "I thought books were the same no matter who's got them."

"It's called the *Shaiféir al Shehn,*" Jeremy answered, "and it's a special book that somebody told me about."

"Your gramps," Sandy said, her voice softening with sympathy.

"Yes," Jeremy replied. "Gramps told me about this book the very last time I saw him. It means *The Book of Life,* and it can help people who are sick like Sara and Zack, or even that drunk guy who tried to mess with me."

"It sounds medical," Sandy murmured.

"Yeah," Jeremy said quickly, "it is, and that's how it can help. Sara's sick, and Zack could be too, and that's not all. What about the other weird stuff that's been happening, like that horrible picture that took over your TV?"

Sandy grabbed Jeremy's arm. "U-ugh," she cried, "that was awful. Those poor people. It was so real, like it wasn't on TV at all."

"It *was* real," Jeremy said, "only it hasn't happened yet."

Sandy's eyes got wider and wider as she stared at him through the gloom of the cave. She lifted her fist to her mouth and began gnawing on the knuckle of her index finger.

"How do you know that?" she whispered, and he felt her trembling. "Jeremy, how do you know all this stuff? Did your gramps tell you?"

"I didn't want to know," he said, "but somebody's got to. It's too complicated, there's not enough time. I'll tell you everything later, I promise."

"Okay," Sandy sighed, "I give up for now—but you'd better tell me later or I'll . . . whatever, you'd better tell me. So, when we get home, I'll get Zack away from you, like you want. After all, it's not like I'd be hurting him or anything."

"You're great, Sandy!" Jeremy whispered.

For a moment, he thought of telling her his worst fear, that he was the one who had hurt Sara. Maybe she'd tell him there was no way he could have, or maybe she'd be totally disgusted and never have anything more to do with him. No, he couldn't risk telling her—it was just too scary. Instead, he put his arm around her, and she looked shyly into his face.

Jeremy thought Sandy might be about to cry, but suddenly she grinned and kissed him quickly on the lips. He blinked as it dawned on him that Sandy actually was a girl. He stood for a second or two, not knowing what to do.

"Now," Sandy said, her grin widening, "can we please get out of this cave?"

Standing up after crouching for so long, they felt faint as they stepped from behind the rock and into the sunlight that spangled the cave mouth. They closed their eyes and held on to each other, teetering on the slanted stone floor. Alaikin's voice sang in Jeremy's memory. "It is the Time of Unbalance, Earth-born, when the seesaw swings wildly on its axis."

Suddenly, Sandy shrieked and flailed her hands in front of her face.

"What is it?" Jeremy yelled, and then something brushed his forehead, something hard and raspy, something that made a squeaky, chittering sound like a crazy laugh.

106

"It's a bat," Sandy yelled, as the creature swirled around them, "a big ugly bat. Jeremy, I hate it! Please, get us out of here."

But now the animal hunched on the floor in front of them, blocking their way. "We'll have to jump over it," Jeremy said grimly.

"Oh no!" Sandy cried, and at that moment Zack stepped into the cave.

"What's all this fuss about," he said, smiling calmly. "It's only a little old bat." He walked over to the creature and bent down to pick it up.

"Zack," Sandy yelled, "don't touch it. You could get rabies!"

"No," Zack said quietly. "It won't bite me." He took the bat behind the wings and lifted it up. "It's my friend."

Zack brought the bat up to his face and stared into its eyes. He whispered something and it chittered back.

"What are you doing?" Jeremy said, shuddering—but he knew even before he asked. Zack and the bat were talking!

The creature's red eyes glittered amid the tangle of light and shadow, and Zack's eyes glared back. Closer and closer their faces came, until Zack suddenly laughed, and with one quick movement launched the bat straight at Jeremy.

Sandy screamed as Jeremy threw up his arm and ducked. Needle-sharp teeth snapped at his head. The bat's claws scrabbled in his hair, but he flailed his arms in a panic and, without intending to, whacked it so hard that it fell to the cave floor. There it lay, stunned and pulsing, glaring up at him.

Loathing flooded Jeremy as he watched the animal pant, seeing, in vivid, slow-motion detail, the wrinkled skin of its belly inflate and sag. He wanted to erase the creature from his sight, to stomp it shapeless in a pool of its own fluids, but he was afraid that it might be quick enough to fasten onto his ankle before he could drive his foot down. He searched the cave for a weapon, and found a large loose rock a few feet away along the back wall. Before he knew it, he'd picked up the rock and held it with both hands above his head, poised to smash it down on the bat.

A cry somewhere between fear and rage tore from Jeremy's throat, like the attack scream of kung fu warriors he had heard in movies but never imagined he could utter. His back arched and his shoulder muscles clenched as he began to drive the rock down.

Then, at the far edge of his vision, Jeremy noticed Zack staring at him greedily, his eyes glowing with bloodlust. For the first time since he'd gone for the rock, Jeremy became fully aware of what he was doing. It was as if, looking at Zack, he saw *himself* in a mirror and was disgusted by what he saw. He looked down at the bat again and saw it not as it was, frightened and bristling, but as it would be if he hit it— pulped and destroyed.

Jeremy began to feel sick. Like an electric shock, it hit him that both the bat and he, at that moment, were being driven by *Ordúrrhg-Zaikh*. But unlike the simple bat, he could think and choose. He could refuse to give way to a flood of loathing and rage, refuse to kill, and try to find another way out.

Jeremy felt the violence drain from him, as a rainstorm, wild in the sky, ends with water seeping quietly into the soil. He lowered the rock and placed it softly on the cave floor.

"It's not your fault," he said to the bat calmly. "I'm sorry I hurt you." Then he reached down to help the bat, which tried to escape, feebly scrabbling its wings and crawling off to one side.

Sandy grabbed Jeremy's arm. "Are you crazy?" she yelled. "Don't touch that thing!" Then she dragged Jeremy around the bat, out of the cave, and into the bright sunlight.

"Did it bite you?" she asked, staring anxiously into his face.

"No," Jeremy said, his knees wobbling a bit. "It missed."

"It wouldn't bite *me*," Zack said, "but it might bite my enemies." He grinned, and the sun glinting off his glasses made his eyes looked like white holes.

"I'm sorry for you, too," Jeremy said, putting his hand on Zack's shoulder. "It can't feel good to be as angry and hateful as you've been lately. I wish you could let all that go and be friends again."

Zack looked startled, as if this were the last thing he'd expected to hear. He shrugged weakly, and his grin faded into a timid smile. Jeremy thought he saw tears welling up behind the shining glasses.

"Zack, it's okay, really," Jeremy said. "I know you can't help it, and I know we *will* be friends when this is all over."

Zack's tentative smile pulled down at the corners and became a grimace of defeat. He pushed Jeremy's hand away, turned, and began to slog back up the path. Jeremy and Sandy followed.

"He looks tired," Jeremy murmured, "all bent over like that drunk guy. I wonder if the Spawn are feeding on his energy."

"Spawn?" Sandy said in a puzzled tone. "Jeremy, what are you talking about?"

Jeremy didn't answer, and Sandy realized she was holding his hand. She started to pull away, but as they caught up to Zack she tightened her grip again.

14 ARE WE THERE YET?

"You kids are awfully quiet," Jeremy's father said when they'd driven a few miles. "Didn't you have a good time?"

"It was okay," Jeremy lied. "Kind of boring. Front Park's better, with the lake. You can go swimming there."

"Yes," his mother said, "but it's almost an hour away, and it's too cold for swimming in October. We'll go there next summer."

It seemed to Jeremy that his father was driving about thirty miles an hour, when the speed limit was fifty-five. Hurry up Dad, he thought to himself, I've got to catch that 3:30 bus! He couldn't help staring at the dashboard clock, even though it was stuck at five past eleven. His watch was broken too. It was supposed to be waterproof, but it hadn't even survived testing in the bathtub.

"Wouldn't it be neat if time stopped when the clock did?" he said to nobody in particular. "Then, if you didn't want something to happen, you could just stop the clock and it wouldn't."

"With a computer," Sandy added, "you could do that too, but then you could fast forward through it or even delete it."

"Too bad the world's not on a computer," Jeremy's mother said, "or maybe that's good because some bad person, or bad *something*, might program it to hurt us, or make a few input errors and crash the system!"

"And if the system crashed," Zack murmured wonderingly, more to himself than anyone else, "everything would blow up and fall to pieces, and we'd all just disappear."

"You guys have the nuttiest ideas," Jeremy's father snorted, shaking his head and smiling. "As the only one in the car with any common sense, the eminent Doctor Taylor says, if I may quote myself, 'get real!'"

Then they rode in silence past a farm on the outskirts of town, where a few spotted dairy cows peacefully chewed their cuds and colts stood head to tail beside their mothers. Jeremy slouched in the back seat next to the window, watching as the somewhat slack telephone wires appeared to rise and fall as the car sped past the poles. The wires reminded him of racehorses, first one and then the next rising up to take the lead and then dropping back as the race went on.

Jeremy wondered how Sara was doing. He still felt bad that she hadn't come on the picnic, but if she had he might never have gotten Sandy alone. Really, he thought, talking to Sandy was more important than Sara's missing some old picnic, because it looked like the only thing that would help Sara at all was if he—and not Zack—found the *Shaiféir al Shehn*. The telephone wires rose and fell. The race went on. Would they never get home?

"Dr. Taylor," Sandy said slowly, "something happened at the park."

"What happened, Sandy?" Jeremy's father replied in a worried tone, as Jeremy reached across Zack to poke Sandy, and Zack caught his wrist. "What was it?"

Sandy bit her lip for a second. "It was in the cave," she blurted. "Jeremy could have got bitten by a bat."

"You rat!" Jeremy yelled.

Zack grinned.

"Jeremy," his father said sternly, "I thought I told you to be careful."

"You didn't actually get bitten, did you, Jer?" his mother asked anxiously.

"No," Jeremy answered, "it just flew really close."

"I'll have to take a good look at you when we get home, Jerry," his father said, sighing. "I guess you can't reasonably expect kids to stay out of trouble," he added to his wife. "If

111

he wasn't actually bitten he'll be all right. But you need to learn to be careful, Jeremy."

"It would have bitten him if it could," Zack said quietly.

"By the way, kids," Jeremy's dad continued, changing to a less disturbing subject and ignoring Zack, "did you know that a long time ago Indians lived in that cave? I'll bet they fished in the creek and collected plants that grew along the banks. They could have used the reeds from the creek to make baskets, and maybe they even grew crops."

"Alright!" Sandy said. "Do you think they had horses, Dr. Taylor, so they could hunt stuff?"

"The Indians didn't get horses until much later, when the Spanish explorers brought them over from Europe. That didn't stop them from hunting, though. Archeologists from the University did some digging around there a few years back, and they found arrowheads and all kinds of animal bones: deer, fox, opossum, dog, you name it."

"You might not know this, guys," Jeremy's mother said, "but there are old Indian drawings on the walls of that cave. I think there are pictures of them in the handout I got last time we went. You can barely see them now, even with a flashlight, but they're still there."

Jeremy's mother opened the glove compartment, pulled out a thin, crumpled pamphlet, and glanced through it. "The drawings are pretty basic," she said, smoothing it against her thigh and handing it to Jeremy, "but you can tell what they were trying to show."

Jeremy took the handout and began to read out loud.

"They do not appear to be pictographs, that is, pictures that serve as writing, like the hieroglyphs of the ancient Egyptians. However, they may have been drawn as part of a ritual to ensure good hunting."

"Wow!" Sandy shouted, leaning across Zack to look at the pamphlet. "There's a guy shooting arrows at a deer, and the deer's got, like, these lines coming out of its neck, arrows or blood or something."

"Check out that one," Zack said with a sneer. "The guy's going to stick a bear with a spear. That's a laugh—it would eat him before he could get close."

"Other pictures," Jeremy continued reading, "may have had religious meaning, or may represent primitive man's attempts to understand the world in which he lived, the vast sky, the sun, moon, and stars."

"Come on, Jeremy," Sandy urged, "turn the page so we can see the rest of the pictures."

As Jeremy reached for the page, he felt a sudden jab of sadness. At last everybody was having fun, but Sara wasn't there to be part of it. And even though he was there, he couldn't really get into it, knowing what he had to do when they got home.

For a moment, he wondered if things would ever be normal again. His heart sank even more when he remembered that nothing could get better unless he managed to complete his mission as *Ouyperkai*. And just how was he going to do that? He had no clue, as usual. He shook his head, took a breath, and tried to pull himself together.

"Come o-o-o-n, Jeremy" Sandy said, rolling her eyes. "Turn the page!"

"Okay, guys, I'm on it," he announced as he flipped the page, and then he forgot everything and simply stared at the picture. Part of the cave wall was covered with stars, drawn with three crossed lines, and a crescent moon. On the other side was the sun, just as he would have done it, a circle with rays of light shooting out in all directions.

And there, at the end of a sun ray longer than any other, he saw a crude etching of a spider with twelve legs. Beneath the moon was a bat-like creature with a fanged mouth and a single huge eye. From the eye, wavy lines went out to two stick-figures of warriors, fighting with spears and clubs.

Alaikin, *Ordúrrg-Zaikh*, and the *Zaikthréem*, Jeremy thought. Even then, the Dragon had brought war and destruction. And Alaikin? Jeremy looked more closely, and noticed

113

that beneath the spider picture was a small, horizontal stick figure with its arms and legs out, as if flying. A carefully carved line surrounded its body.

Dimshen-cardác, Jeremy thought—Travel-on—and his skin tingled faintly with an echo of the golden shield that had protected him on his journey beyond Space and Time. Further down was a small group of figures sitting in a circle. Their hands were joined, and there was not a weapon among them.

"What's the matter with you," snarled Zack, breaking Jeremy's trance. "Are you getting car-sick? Should we stop and let little Jeremy out before he pukes all over the place? Those pictures are all screwed up anyway. Spiders don't have twelve legs and bats don't have one eye. Those Indians didn't know what they were doing."

"Zack, what's bothering you?" said Jeremy's mother. "You seem pretty grumpy for a kid who's just been on a picnic."

"We're home!" Jeremy's father announced, pulling into the driveway. "Come on in, Jer—I'll make sure the bat didn't bite you."

"Aw, Dad," Jeremy said, "it only brushed my hair a little."

"Jeremy . . ."

"Oh, all right," Jeremy said, "check me over, but don't take too long, okay? I need to go out and do some stuff."

Jeremy followed his dad into the house, wishing he'd said nothing about going out. Zack had headed home quickly to avoid having to answer his mom's question, but when he heard what Jeremy said he stopped and glanced back.

All the way up the front steps, Jeremy had felt Zack's eyes bore into his back. He thought of the bat, probably clinging upside-down to the cave top with its wicked claws, red eyes staring into the dark. Jeremy shuddered and bit his lip. Sandy would have a hard time getting rid of her brother now that he had stupidly tipped Zack off. When would he learn to think before blurting out something that got him in trouble?

15 WHAT JUST HAPPENED (AGAIN)?

"Dad, we're back," Sandy shouted as she opened the front door.

"Okay, honey," her father answered from his office at the back of the house. "Say, would you and Zack come in here for a minute?"

"Sure," she answered, noting that he sounded puzzled. Something must be on his mind, because he never allowed them in his office when he was working.

"Did you guys have a good time?" he asked.

"It was okay," Sandy answered, her words spilling out quickly to hide what she wasn't saying. "There were paths in the woods and this Indian cave only we didn't know it was until Jeremy's mom told us."

"How about you, Zack?" their father asked. "You've been pretty quiet lately. Everything okay?"

"No wonder you think I'm quiet," Zack shot back, "you hardly talk to me. There's nothing *wrong* with me, if that's what you mean."

Mr. Tatum sighed and put his hand on Zack's arm. "Look, big guy, I'm sorry I've been so busy. After I finish this project I'll help you with your program, that dinosaur-battle thing."

"Dino-Battle's finished, Dad," Zack answered, "as much as it can be on that fossil computer you make me use. It's got, like, zero memory. If you'd let me on your system, I could really do something."

"Zack," Mr. Tatum groaned, "you can be the most exasperating kid. Fifty times I've told why you can't use my system. I can't take a chance my work files will get screwed up. Now,

115

I've spent a lot of time teaching you to program, but you don't seem to appreciate that."

"Yeah, sure," Zack replied sullenly. "Thanks a bunch. As if I *could* screw up your system! Your files are pass-word protected and encoded. I'd have to do some serious hacking."

"You *haven't* done that, have you, Zack?" Mr. Tatum said slowly. "The system's been real glitchy lately."

"Come on, Dad," Zack answered, "You'd kill me if I messed with your files."

"Maybe it's the electricity," Sandy said. "The TV's been switching channels, and I told you about that weird picture, right, that came out of nowhere? You said it was the weather or some sort of interference."

"No," Mr. Tatum answered, "there's something more going on, but darned if I know what. Look how this one program got corrupted." He typed for a few seconds and then slammed his fist on the table.

"Damn," he muttered. "What's that? I didn't call that—it just took over! Some of it's mine, but what's the rest of that garbage?"

"It's some weird kind of graphics," Zack said, staring at the screen, "but it's changing too fast to get a good look."

Mr. Tatum whistled and shook his head. "I can't believe it!" he muttered. "This has never happened before. Wait—it's slowing down."

"Dad!" Sandy yelled, grabbing her father's arm. "I know that one. It's from the Indian cave. Jeremy's mom just showed us!"

"What the . . . ?" Mr. Tatum, whispered, his eyes widening in surprise.

"Yeah," Zack said softly, staring at the screen. "There's the bat picture, with that wavy stuff *pouring* out of its eye, and the spider thing zigzagging all over the place."

"Hold on," Mr. Tatum said, "it's changing again. Those look like Egyptian hieroglyphs. There's that eye thing—and the bug, what do they call it?"

"The eye of Horus, Dad," Zack said, "and the scarab beetle. Jeremy told me about them."

"And what's that?" Sandy shouted, pointing at the screen. "Wait, now it's gone blank. It was like the plan of a building. Did you see it, Zack?"

"Yeah," Zack muttered, "but it was too fast to tell what it was."

"Oh, come on," Sandy said. "You're supposed to have a photographic memory, so *remember*."

Sandy watched Zack close his eyes and concentrate. She had seen something like an architect's drawing, with a bright, flashing light on the left side. But none of the labels had stuck in her mind, so she had no idea what it actually was.

"It's not happening again," her father said, clicking away on the keyboard, "and only my files show up in the directory. Whatever was there, it's gone now."

Zack opened his eyes and grinned slyly. "I know what it was," he said.

"What?" Sandy and their father both asked at once.

"It's the Museum of Natural History," Zack answered. "The basement plan and the first floor. That's what the label said."

"Zack, your memory is incredible!" his father exclaimed, patting him on the shoulder. "My dad's was too—I guess it skipped a generation. But what was that flashing thing?"

"I don't know," Zack said slowly. "It didn't have any label. Maybe the location of something?"

Sandy gnawed on a knuckle as she tried to keep up with her rushing thoughts. The Museum! Jeremy's book! Had Zack guessed everything? But he couldn't know that Jeremy was actually going to the Museum, and she had to keep it that way.

"I just don't get it," Mr. Tatum said, shaking his head in disgust. "It's not a virus. Maybe some hotshot hacker got past the security and is jerking people around for fun. Or it could be an Internet router had a partial crash, spliced and diced some files, and sent them everywhere. Pretty scary! Anyway, you kids need to clear out. I'm so far behind I'll be up half the night.

Can you get your own dinner? There's stuff in the freezer, just stick it in the microwave."

* * *

Dr. Taylor examined every inch of Jeremy's scalp. Then he looked into his ears and nose with a pocket flashlight.

"Stop squirming," he said, "or I'll have to tie you up like an Indian."

"You and what army?" Jeremy joked, faking a punch at his dad, who pretended to duck. It was one of many fun routines they'd worked out over the years to blow off a little steam without either getting angry. Then Jeremy kept as still as he could until, at last, his dad put the flashlight away, brushed his hands on his coat, and patted him on the back of the head.

"Okay, scram," he said. "I'll send you my bill."

"Sure," Jeremy said, laughing. "And I'll send it back. See you later . . ."

There was still a little time before the bus, and Jeremy didn't want to wait at the stop, where Zack might be lurking. He went to his room, sat on his bed, and gazed out the window into the yard. The sky had cleared while they were at the park, but now clouds were moving in again, and it looked like an evening storm was on the way.

Pulling the ankh from his pocket, Jeremy rubbed his thumb slowly over the stone, tracing the loop again and again. As the colors of the *Zhystrém Haistrál* tinged his skin, he started to feel better about things. Surely, Alaikin would come to help at the Museum. The Arkanian couldn't expect him to take on *Ordúrrg-Zaikh* alone, could he?

On the inside of Jeremy's door, guarding his room, was a present from Grandpa Heinrich: a circular Egyptian canvas with sewn-on figures. Around the canvas was a fringe held on

118

by tiny, hand-made stitches, and at the center two gods poured holy oil over a prince. This ceremony was called anointing the pharaoh, Grandpa Heinrich had explained, and it meant the pharaoh was now accepted by the gods.

Each god actually looked like a man with a mask. One was Horus the Hawk and the other was Anubis the Jackal. The anointing oil came down in a wavy black line all around the prince, reminding Jeremy of the golden shield of *Dimshencardác.*

"Alaikin will come, won't he?" he murmured out loud.

"Maybe, if you r-r-really need him," Cleopatra purred as she glided through the bedroom door. "But you're doing pr-r-r-etty well by yourself, for a human."

She jumped gracefully onto his bed. Jeremy stroked her head slowly, pulling her ears back and down. He loved it when they automatically popped up again, as if each had a built-in spring, as his hand left them and flowed down the rest of her body to the tip of her tail.

"You certainly know how to tr-r-eat a gir-r-rl," she thought deliriously, and then flopped onto her side to have her belly rubbed.

Cleo looked so sweet and ecstatic, her eyes glowing and her purr revving to its deepest and strongest level, that Jeremy simply couldn't stand it. Impulsively, he put his face next to hers and blew gently into her ear. He knew she didn't like this, but he couldn't resist teasing her, just as he couldn't help teasing Sara. Cleo shook her head, jumped to her feet, and glared at him, growling crossly.

"Whatever Zack has," she thought, "you're catching it." She put her front paws on his thigh and stretched, flexing her claws so they pricked lightly through his jeans. "Before you get any other bright ideas, isn't it time you left?" she thought, swishing her tail. "You've got a date at the Museum, and I've got better things to do than amuse you."

"I'm sorry, Cleo," Jeremy thought back. "I don't know what comes over me. It's just, sometimes you look so relaxed and pleased with yourself that I can't help messing with you."

Jeremy giggled as Cleo stuck in her claws a bit harder, until he could feel their business ends penetrate the topmost layer of his skin. She was gazing into his eyes, though, and when they widened with surprise, she relaxed her grip again.

"Consider this a warning," she thought, and Jeremy didn't know whether she meant the more forceful probing of her claws or whatever she was going to say next. Maybe both.

"Watch out for Zack," she continued. "From what I see of your memories, he's on to you. That bat told him something in the cave and I'll bet he's guessed a lot more."

"The bat!" Jeremy whispered. "I thought they were talking. *Ordúrrg-Zaikh* gets everywhere, doesn't he?"

"Everywhere but her-r-re," she purred, licking the fur on her chest. "Be careful, Jeremy. I don't know about Alaikin, but I may be able to help you."

"How could you help," Jeremy thought. "You'll be taking your afternoon nap on the windowsill, snoozing in the sunlight, as usual."

If cats can smile, Cleo did exactly that. Jeremy shook his head, grinned back at her, and patted her once more before he stood up. He wanted to hold onto this last quiet moment before plunging again into danger. Cleo's fur crackled slightly, as if with static electricity.

"Energy from the *Zhystrém Haistrál*," she thought, "caught in the ankh. Don't forget this ally, Jeremy. Good luck, and before you leave, be a sweet boy and put something tasty in my dish? I'd love a snack before my nap."

As Jeremy took some cat treats from the box, his mother called from the back yard. "Jerry, are you going out?"

"Yeah, Mom," he answered. "I'm not real sure when I'll be back. I've got stuff to do."

"As long as you're back by six o'clock. I'm making something special for dinner."

"See you later," Jeremy yelled back.

Yes, he thought, but how much later? Whatever happened at the Museum, it wouldn't be a picnic.

Jeremy poked his head out the front door and looked around. No Zack. Sandy must have done it! He walked quickly to the bus stop, hunching his shoulders as if to shrink himself into invisibility.

Now would be a nice time to be able to stop the clock, he thought. Zack would be stuck, and he could breeze past everybody, find the *Shaiféir al Shehn*, and do what had to be done. Then he might *really* get back in time for Mom's special dinner.

16 FOX AND RABBIT

Jeremy let himself relax just a bit as he slipped into a seat toward the center of the bus. There had been no sign of Zack around the bus stop, even behind the hedge along the sidewalk.

Hurray for Sandy, he thought, wondering how she'd gotten her brother out of the way. She didn't know what he knew, but she sure was helping. Jeremy wondered if she might be a Guardian of some sort even if she didn't know everything. Maybe there were different types of *Ouyperkain* with different levels of knowledge, like different levels of a video game. Mr. MacIvery could be one too.

A few seats in front of Jeremy sat two old ladies, and he couldn't help overhearing what they said.

"Mary Beth, you could of knocked me over with a feather," said the most ancient one, shaking her head so its white curls bobbed softly. Her nose twitched as if she were trying to stop a sneeze. She peeked timidly out of a heavy winter coat, and Jeremy thought she looked like a scared white rabbit.

"I've never known Arthur to behave like that," she continued, "not in all the years. He looked like he was going to hit me! *Me*, his own mother. His eyes were blazing mad—like that awful man in the movies, what's his name?"

"Vin Diesel?" asked the younger of the two, who was still quite old. Her hair was salt and pepper colored, and she had a very long nose with a ledge in the middle that made her look, unfortunately for her, a lot like Mr. MacIvery. Around her coat collar a fox skin curled, as if she didn't know or didn't care that fur stoles were sixty years out of style.

The dead animal's head hung over the seatback so that, above sharp teeth, its glassy brown eyes stared right at Jeremy. He couldn't help thinking of Zack's teeth, bared in the nasty white grin he so often wore lately, and of the needle-sharp teeth of the bat. Clenching his own teeth, he hunched down in his seat as if the creature were about to fly at his head again.

"Yep," the rabbity lady was saying. "That's him, Vin Diesel. That hoodlum who is always hitting somebody or shooting somebody or doing something nasty. Sometimes he's supposed to be forced to do it, for the good of others. Well, I do wish somebody in the movies would be forced to do something *nice* for the good of others."

"Mother," said the lady with the fox, "did you do anything at all to make Arthur mad?"

"Of course not," answered her mother. "I just asked him how he was feeling. You know how he's been so irritable lately? Well, he glared at me—there's no other word for it—he simply *glared*. Why, his eyes were just red with fury."

"So you came right over to me?" the daughter continued.

"What else was I *to* do, Mary Beth," said the mother, wrinkling her nose in a rabbity way. "He scared the living daylights out of me."

"Well, we'll take care of *him*," said Mary Beth. She stuck out her jaw, and Jeremy thought she looked a little like the fox she wore. "I'm not going to let anybody act like that toward my mama. Not even brother Arthur, drat his ignorant heart."

"Mary Beth, it's more than just Arthur," said the mother. She brushed a tear from her cheek. "People everywhere are so hateful lately, I don't know what to make of it. Seems like everybody's gone and caught rabies or something. Maybe it's just winter coming on."

"There, there, Mama," said Mary Beth, kissing her on the cheek. "Don't you fret. Mary Beth will take care of everything."

Jeremy sat very still, wondering about the "Arthur" they spoke of. Had the *Zaikhthréem* gotten to Arthur too? He imagined how the Fox Lady's brother would look, maybe fox-faced like her, but with glinting red eyes. Then the hair on his neck prickled, as if those eyes were staring at him from behind. He tried to keep still, but his head began to turn.

Slowly, as if someone were pulling him with a rope, Jeremy turned right around. From the back seat, his eyes boring into Jeremy's and his teeth white as the fox's, Zack grinned.

Jeremy got up and walked stiffly toward the back of the bus. He felt as if somebody else were walking his body—as if he were a puppet and Zack pulled the strings.

"How . . . how?" Jeremy stammered as he sat down in the back seat.

"Sandy really did her best, Jeremy," Zack said brightly. "She got me a long way from your house and from the bus stop. But she forgot there were other stops before yours. So when the bus came, I got on. You should have seen the look on her face!"

"Then you knew I was going," Jeremy said. "But how? And why didn't I see you when I got on the bus?"

"I'm supposed to know things," Zack smirked. "I'm a genius, remember? And you didn't see me because I was out of sight." Zack hunched down until he was hidden by the seat in front of him.

He knows where I'm going, Jeremy thought, but maybe he doesn't know why.

"Of course I do," Zack said, popping back up in his seat.

"Do *what*?" Jeremy nearly shouted.

"Know why," Zack said calmly. "I know exactly why you're going to the Museum."

Jeremy felt his eyes growing rounder and rounder, filling with fear like balloons filling up with water. He couldn't turn off the tap, and the flow went on. Was Zack reading his mind?

"Don't look so scared, little Jeremy," Zack smirked. "We can't read your mind—not *yet*. I was at the antique shop, remember? When that MacIvery fool didn't have *The Book of Life*, it wasn't hard to guess you'd go to the Museum to find it.

Sometimes you are awfully slow, Jeremy Taylor. When will you figure out that we function at a much higher level than you?"

"*We?*" Jeremy questioned, dreading the answer. "Who's *we?*"

"You mean you really don't know?" Zack said, grabbing Jeremy's wrist. "*We* are the ones who want to know *why* you want that book. Tell us, Jeremy!"

Zack's grip on Jeremy's wrist grew stronger and stronger, like a pipe wrench cranked tighter and tighter. His eyes bored into Jeremy's like icicles, until Jeremy's head hurt almost as much as his wrist. He tried to break Zack's hold, but Zack was too strong, far stronger than he should have been.

"Zack," Jeremy pleaded, "you're hurting me. Stop it or you'll break my wrist!"

For a moment Zack looked stunned, as though Jeremy had slapped him. Then, his grip loosened and his face screwed up with shame.

"I . . . we . . . I," he stammered, as the red glint in his eye flickered on and off like a failing neon sign. Tears brimmed over his eyelids and streaked his face.

"Fight, Zack," Jeremy whispered. "You are Zack Tatum, and you *can* beat the Spawn if you fight them. I'm your friend, your blood brother—you don't want to hurt me. Sandy and Charley and Sara, we're all your friends. We'll help you!"

Zack looked completely bewildered. "Jeremy?" he asked softly, "What's wrong? Why am I crying?"

Jeremy pulled the ankh from his pocket and held it out to Zack. The colors of the *Zhystrém Haistrál* pulsed brightly on the stone. Never had Jeremy seen anybody do two opposite things at once, but now Zack did. His whole body shrank from the ankh, but his right hand crept toward it. He looked like a little kid whose mother has warned him not to take candy from strangers.

Somebody pulled the cord to stop the bus. The buzzer rasped in Jeremy's ears. Startled, he took his eyes off Zack and glanced toward the front door.

"Stop here, Driver," yelped the lady with the fox, pulling the buzzer cord again and again. "Right here! I told you Crescent Circle—why didn't you stop?"

"Okay, lady," the driver said disgustedly. "The stop is on the far side of the intersection, and you have to get off at the stop."

"Nonsense," she snapped. "You forgot, and you're trying to make excuses. You're reckless! I should report you, for a reckless driver."

"Okay," the driver muttered again. "Have it your way, I forgot. It's only a few feet back to the street."

The two women shuffled off the bus, and Jeremy turned back to Zack. Instantly, he knew he'd lost him. The smug, superior grin was back, and his voice was cold and mocking.

"Your little toy's not working so hot," Zack said, sneering at the ankh. "You might as well ditch it, for all the good it's gonna do you."

The ankh was dull, as if its shimmering colors were covered by a layer of rust, and the red light gleamed steadily in Zack's eyes.

Sadly, Jeremy raised his arm and pulled the cord for a stop. The bus whooshed to the curb. As Jeremy pushed out the door, Zack grabbed his jacket, breathing down his neck.

17 ARE WE HAVING FUN YET?

"Almost closing time," the Museum guard said as Jeremy bought his ticket. He hesitated for a moment and then got another one for Zack.

The stooped, ancient guard looked Jeremy up and down. "Hey!" he exclaimed suddenly. "Aren't you the kid that used to come in with old Heinrich Heller? Grew up some, didn't you?"

"Yes," Jeremy replied. "Heinrich Heller was my grandfather. My name's Jeremy Taylor, and this is my friend Zack."

"Well, well," the old man continued. "I was real sorry to hear about your grandpa, Jeremy. He got a big write-up in the *Times*. Left us a bunch of stuff too, that just came in a few weeks ago."

"Mister," Jeremy asked hopefully, "could you tell me where I could see that stuff?"

"Oh, gosh," the guard answered, rubbing his stubbled chin. "I don't think they've even got round to cataloging all that, much less putting it out. No room for it, anyhow."

"So there's no way I could look at it?" Jeremy insisted, his heart sinking. "It's pretty important to me, especially since my Gramps died and all."

"Well," the old man answered, scratching his scalp through wisps of white hair. "I see what you mean, but like I told you, it's all down in storage—I'm not even sure where. I could ask the Director if she was here, but she went on vacation."

Jeremy felt as if the floor had opened up beneath him. No way, he thought to himself—there's just no way. Grandpa Heinrich was dead, the *Shaiféir al Shehn* was beyond reach, and everything was hopeless. He felt sick and his body started trembling.

"You'll only get tougher if you fight the odds," he remembered his father saying. "But he's only a kid," his mother had replied. She was *so* right, he was only a kid.

Suddenly, Zack pushed in front of Jeremy and shoved his face right at the guard's. "Come on!" Zack demanded, "can't you see he really misses his grandpa? Why don't you just tell us where that stuff is?"

"Whoa there, sonny," the guard answered. "Hold your horses. Didn't I just tell you that I don't know where anything is? I'm sorry about Mr. Heller too, but that don't change anything. You boys best come back in a month or so, when they get everything sorted out. What's your hurry, anyhow?"

"No hurry, Mister," Jeremy said miserably, wishing Zack really wanted to help him, but knowing he was only after the *Shaiféir al Shehn.* "I just felt kind of lonely to see something of Gramps's. But I guess we can come back."

"You do that, then," the guard replied. "Even if it's still in storage, I'll bet the Director would show it to you."

"Yeah," Jeremy said, his voice rising with excitement as a plan took shape in his mind. "Mrs. Dart's a neat lady. I met her once with Grandpa Heinrich, and she showed us all kinds of things that regular people don't get to see.

"Hey, is there time for my friend and me to see some of the stuff that *is* on display?"

"Better hurry up," the guard said, checking his watch. "We close in twenty minutes."

"Come on," Jeremy said, tugging Zack by the sleeve. "Let's look at the Egyptian exhibit."

"Just don't be running," the guard said. "You can't see the whole Museum in twenty minutes, can you?"

"Yes Sir, I mean no Sir," Jeremy said, and as he showed Zack the way he heard the old man give a chuckle that ended in a brief snort.

Jeremy and Zack approached the high-point of the Egyptian display, a full-scale replica of the tomb of an Egyptian pharaoh. Everything was copied exactly as it had been discovered, except for the real mummy in its actual coffin—a huge sarcophagus. Above a narrow staircase that led down into the tomb, the Museum had placed the sign "Enter Only," and from the other side steps led up to an exit.

"They took out his insides and put in spices to keep him from rotting," Jeremy said, thinking furiously as they climbed down the stairs. For all he knew, Zack might be strong enough now to actually read his mind, so he had to cover up what he was really thinking with a lot of distracting mental noise.

"Then they wrapped him up. After he died, of course. But the sarcophagus is the neatest part. It's got three layers, wood on the outside and the inside one is pure gold. Come on, I'll show you."

The lids to each of the three layers of the sarcophagus were open, showing the cloth-wrapped mummy inside. "See, on the outside lid," Jeremy said, "how they've painted his arms crossed? He's holding an ankh, just like the one Grandpa Heinrich gave me, and his other hand's got the flail—what they used after the harvest to get the husks off their wheat. The pharaoh holds the flail, and that shows he's the king, provider for all of the people."

Jeremy went on chattering and pointing, all the time devising ways to shake Zack, who stuck to him like a leech. His plan for finding the *Shaiféir al Shehn* wasn't much, but it wasn't anything if he couldn't get rid of Zack.

Should he trip him and push him over, and then run out before he got back up? A TV detective had done that once when some bad guy was following him. But Zack had grown too strong for that to work.

What about throwing something into Zack's eyes, to blind him just long enough to get away? But Jeremy saw no dust or dirt anywhere. He wondered what his dad would say. "Go for it," probably, and "if you lose, just learn from your opponent and beat him the next time."

Jeremy had heard that so many times that his brain repeated it automatically, but just *how* should he go for it? It felt bad to be thinking of ways to hurt Zack. Even if the *Zaikhthréem* had him, he was still a friend and, like Jeremy himself, just a kid. In his mind, he heard his mother's voice say that, and he found himself thinking in reply.

After all, he reasoned, I decided not to hurt the bat, even though it was far more disgusting than Zack. So no way should I have to hurt him, right? But time was running out, and he had to get to the *Shaiféir al Shehn* alone. Zack might once have been just a kid, but now he was a lot more, and losing and learning were not an option. This might be the only game he got, and he *had* to win. He kept on talking to keep Zack busy, but all the while his mind was planning.

"Check out the paintings near the door, Zack. There's the scarab, this beetle that was supposed to guide the pharaoh on his journey after death. And that thing with the sharp corners that looks like a picture of a football is the Eye of Horus. He was this god who was the son of Osiris. Another god named Seth tore Osiris to pieces, but then Horus killed Seth. The Egyptians thought the pharaoh was like Osiris, so they put the Eye of Horus on his tomb to guard against evil."

Zack had been quiet, but now his hard, flat voice suddenly echoed in the tomb. "You can stop the tour now, Jeremy. I know you're just thinking of a way to get that book—and for me *not* to get it. Save yourself the trouble. Horus stopped us once, but not this time."

"What are you saying?" Jeremy exclaimed. "You're talking crazy, Zack, like you actually *are* Seth!"

"Yes," Zack said, a strange smile taking over his face. "And you talk as if you *are* Horus. Or don't you recognize yourself yet?"

"Hey," Jeremy answered, "stop acting so spooky. I'm your friend and I'm telling you that none of this Horus and Seth stuff is real. It's just stories made up by people who've been dead for thousands of years!"

Zack grabbed Jeremy by the shoulders and stared at him. Jeremy tried to twist away from his red, probing eyes, but Zack's grip was as strong as steel.

"You're the one who's crazy," Zack said in a voice as dead as a mummy's. "You can't even see what's in front of your eyes and you won't even hear what goes into your ears. All right then. We'll *make* you see and we'll make you hear."

A mocking laugh echoed through the tomb. It came from Zack's mouth, but it was not his laugh, just as the strength in the grip on Jeremy's shoulders came from Zack's hands but was not his. Zack's glowing eyes soaked up the light in the tomb until those eyes were all Jeremy could see. A wave of darkness washed over him, and only Zack's hold kept him from crumpling to the floor.

Two voices, neither Zack's nor Jeremy's, seemed to come from the very walls of the tomb. One, low and powerful like an organ, he'd heard in the cave of *Ordúrrg-Zaikh*. The other, dancing around the edges of the first, had the chiming tone of the *Zhystrém Haistrál*. Both voices spoke a poem, and Jeremy listened.

> Nothing that lives will die.
> Nothing that dies is dead.
> Gods and Guardians,
> Dragon and Spawn,
> All are here,
> None is gone.

> Return, Seth, the Destroyer.
> Return, Horus, the Avenger.
> Though names may change
> The struggle remains.
> The battle forever begun
> Will never be lost and never won.

131

Suddenly, two huge shadows loomed on the wall of the tomb, locked in combat. Horus, with a human body and the head of a hawk, grappled with the hideous form of *Ordúrrg-Zaikh*. The creature's huge tail coiled around Horus's neck and thrust him down, while its claws gripped his legs. Back and back bent Horus under the monstrous weight, until it seemed he must break in half. But the Hawk fought back, stabbing and snapping his beak at the *Zaikhthréem* that swarmed over him and slashing at the Dragon's huge red eye.

The shapes on the wall of the tomb shimmered and shifted. Now Jeremy saw not Seth and Horus, but huge images of Zack and himself wrestling each other, just as they actually were. Zack was right. Jeremy could no longer deny what he saw and heard. He knew who he was fighting, and he knew who would win unless he fought harder.

"Nobody is going to hand it to you," his dad's voice sounded in his head. "You've got to earn it."

And yet, even with everything at stake, Jeremy couldn't do it. His legs turned rubbery and the familiar sick feeling gripped his stomach. He was no good at fighting, never was and never would be. So how was he to win against a creature as strong as Zack had become? This was not fair. Far too much was expected of him.

"Help!" he thought as loudly as he could. "Alaikin!" But there was no answer, even as he felt himself begin to give way.

"You'll only get tougher if you fight the odds," his father's voice rose again from his memory, "not if you get a cheap break." Jeremy's knees buckled and he folded, kneeling to the floor.

Human voices sounded from the top of the stairs. The patter of little children's footsteps approached the entrance to the tomb. "Hurry up, class," a tired teacher called out. "But stay together and don't run on the stairs. We have only five minutes to see the tomb."

"Oh boy, oh boy," piped several scampering kids. "The mummy! We're gonna see the mummy!"

The giant images faded from the wall and Zack, distracted by the unexpected company, loosened his grip. Cheap break or just dumb luck, Jeremy knew this would be his only chance. He wasn't anywhere near as strong as Zack, but maybe, this time, he could be smarter. And he knew for sure that he was faster. Maybe this was the lesson he needed to learn in order to win—not to try to fight strength with strength but to use the weapons he had.

He pulled himself together, took a breath, and before Zack could react, threw up his arms and ducked down and away, leaving his empty jacket in Zack's clenched fists. In a split-second, Jeremy spun around and ran full speed up the entrance steps.

As he raced away, he began to feel a new confidence, a sense that even though he had messed up so many times, he might finally succeed after all. If he had gotten a cheap break with the kids showing up out of nowhere, at least he'd learned enough to take advantage of it. He pushed his way past the kids and burst out of the tomb just as their teacher reached the stairs.

"What rudeness!" the teacher yelled at him as he rushed past. "You come back here and apologize, young man, right now!"

Jeremy turned and saw that Zack was stuck, halfway up the stairs, behind a solid wall of little kids. His face was twisted with hate, but as Jeremy turned away again he saw that hatred fade to loneliness.

At that moment, he felt so sorry for Zack that he had an urge to wait for him. It was nuts, just as when he'd reached down to help the poor bat in the cave. But Sandy'd had the sense to stop him then, and now he had the sense to stop himself. Just because you felt sorry for somebody didn't mean you had to let them hurt you.

Jeremy thought of Horus, pressed to breaking by the weight of *Ordúrrg-Zaikh*, and he felt the pain and numbness left by Zack's harsh grip. Zack might be just a kid, and a pretty pathetic one at that, but he was also dangerous, and giving him a loving hug wouldn't help. There was only one way to help Zack, and everyone else, and that was for Jeremy to complete his task.

"Excuse me," he blurted at the teacher over his shoulder as he broke into a run.

"Get back here, you rotten kid!" she shouted, staring after him and pointing her finger. There was no reply. "No manners whatsoever," she muttered in disgust as she turned and started down the stairs.

Then, as Zack's feet pounded up the exit stairway on the other side, she asked in a puzzled tone "Who's there?"

18 THE BATTLE BEGUN

"I don't see how I missed those kids," the old Museum guard muttered to himself as he started to lock up. "But I swear I didn't see them go out." He jingled his keys, scratched his chin, and peered around the lobby.

"Closing time," he shouted, and his voice echoed from the marble walls. "Last chance, everybody out!"

"Hmmm," he said to the answering silence. "Maybe they went out when I took my break—or was that before they got here? Better check those restrooms again."

He went to the back of the lobby and into the Men's Room. "Anybody in here?" he yelled, walking down the row of stalls and pushing open the doors. "I guess not."

He opened the door to the Ladies Room, quickly glanced inside, and yelled again. "Nobody home," he muttered, "though boys shouldn't be in *there* anyway. Well, they'd better be out, or they'll be mighty hungry by morning." He switched off the light and walked back to the front door.

Crouching on the toilet seat in the farthest stall of the Ladies Room, Jeremy heard the guard's footsteps fade and the bolt to the brass front doors snap shut. The sound echoed through the gloom like a rifle shot. Then came silence, and more silence.

Jeremy felt as if he'd had to stay after school and even the teacher had gone home. The huge building loomed around him. A deep rumbling came from far below, as if he'd been swallowed by an enormous animal now getting ready to digest him.

When he realized that the sound was only the furnace coming on, Jeremy started breathing again. He felt so alone that he almost wished Zack *would* find him. But Zack wasn't his friend any more. Zack wasn't even Zack any more. Jeremy still felt the powerful grip on his shoulders, the aching bruises where Zack had grabbed him in the tomb. No, he had to go on by himself. The task was his, and at least for now it was his alone.

"You'll only get tougher if you fight the odds," his father's voice rumbled at him again from the depths of his mind.

It's nice to hear from dear old Dad again, Jeremy thought, but sometimes he just repeats the obvious. He knew his dad loved him and worried about him, but having been in the military he had this "tough guy" attitude toward life, or so his mom said, and he believed this was the best way for his son too.

A small, rebellious grin snuck onto Jeremy's face as he thought back at the familiar voice, Yeh, Dad, I know—nobody's going to hand me anything—you said that a few times already. Like a hundred times, he continued to himself.

Then he stepped quietly down to the tile floor and stretched his cramped legs. He felt something warm in his pants pocket and pulled out the ankh. Gone was the rusty coating that had dulled it after he and Zack had clashed on the bus. The colors of the *Zhystrém Haistrál* again played over the stone and glowed on his hand.

He felt better, but still utterly alone. He closed his eyes and folded both hands around the ankh. "Alaikin?" he thought with all his might. "Spider, where are you?"

For a moment, Jeremy felt as if he were floating in space, warmed by the golden light of *Dimshen-cardác*. Alaikin's melody sang faintly in his mind, as if it came from very far away.

"Sorry, old chap," the Arkanian whispered, "a bit occupied at the moment." Jeremy stared wildly around the stall, but Alaikin was nowhere to be seen. The song faded, and the next words were like a barely remembered dream.

"Trouble on the far side of the galaxy!"

Jeremy had to force himself to walk, as if his feet were sticking in mud. The rush of confidence he'd felt after escaping Zack had drained away, and he was mired in his usual indecision.

What to do next? So much depended on the course he chose, but he didn't have a clue. Well, he'd come pretty far not knowing what to do, so despite that maybe he'd get even further.

Jeremy wished he could keep on hiding and let someone else deal with things, but that wouldn't help Sara, and anyway if Zack got to the *Shaiféir al Shehn* first, there'd be no place to hide from *Ordúrrg-Zaikh*. No way would the Dragon *let* him win. This time, his dad's advice was right. He'd have to earn it.

Jeremy took a deep breath and pushed out of the dimness of the rest room. The last light of the sun was setting the lobby's white marble on fire.

It's beautiful, he thought as he padded quickly across the large expanse, straining his ears and glancing in every direction. The sight of such glory gave him new hope and strength. With loveliness like this in the world, how could evil win?

Jeremy thought of home, warm and happy, as it was before all the trouble began. He realized that at that moment his mom would be starting their special dinner, and maybe wondering where he was. If she could see the fix he was in now, she'd want to hug him until all his worries melted away.

That would make him feel a whole lot better, but it wouldn't do a thing to stop *Ordúrrg-Zaikh*. He swallowed against the lump forming in his throat and made himself keep walking.

The guard had said that Grandpa Heinrich's things were "down" in storage, so Jeremy planned to search the basement first. The door to the stairs was locked. He pressed the elevator button, and felt his heart pound in his throat as its doors slowly opened.

Zack leaped out from a dozen angles—all imagined. The elevator was empty, though now, from its sound, Zack *would* know exactly where he was.

AUTHORIZED PERSONNEL ONLY!

read the sign next to the basement button. "I hereby author-ize myself," Jeremy thought, pressing the button and smiling.

This was the sort of thing Grandpa Heinrich would say, and it made him feel a little braver. He remembered some-thing Gramps had once told him while explaining an Egyptian fable about a lion and a jackal.

"Being brave doesn't always mean roaring and forcing your way through. It can mean having the guts to believe in your-self, in your plans, and carry them out even if someone stronger stands in the way. The jackal won because he admit-ted to himself that he was weaker than the lion, so he knew he had to be smarter. The dumb, strong lion, poor thing, had no clue."

Okay, Jeremy said to himself, I'll stick to my plan—once I have one. Even so, as the elevator crept slowly downward, his stomach crept steadily up toward his throat. He swallowed hard, ready to run when the doors opened. Run like hell—I guess that's my plan for now, he thought, and smiled grimly at his own joke.

A row of glassed-in offices stretched in both directions. He turned right and crept down a dim, creaking corridor as qui-etly as he could, thankful he was wearing sneakers. The hair on the back of his neck twitched.

Watch out! Go back! his mind screamed, but he went on.

At corridor's far end was a door marked STORAGE. Jeremy turned the handle and pushed, but it wouldn't budge. He tried again, pushing harder. The door fought him, but squeaked slowly open against a stiff spring. He wedged it with his foot and, staring into darkness, felt along the wall for a light switch.

Cool, musty air pressed against his face, air that smelled as if it might have been waiting for centuries. It feels like the Indian cave, he thought, but at least there won't be bats. And please, he prayed, nothing worse!

His hand found the switch and flipped it. Fluorescent lights flickered on, revealing row after row of broad metal shelves mounted in racks five or six feet apart. Each rack stretched from the floor to a ceiling that had to be nearly twenty feet high.

On the shelves were stacked labeled boxes of all sizes, and a clutter of assorted objects wrapped in brown paper or clear plastic. The room was huge. How could he find Grandpa Heinrich's things in such a forest of stuff? They might be at the very top, buried in the middle, or shoved under the bottom of any of the rows of shelves.

Jeremy eased the door closed and crept slowly past the first few rows, peering around the corners of the racks. Each row had a built-in sliding ladder on both sides, mounted on a rail that ran along the top, so even the highest shelves could be reached. He'd seen something like it in a movie, an old library with sliding ladders.

It would be really neat to climb up the ladder, he thought, kick away from the end, and glide down the whole row, like they'd done in the film. But how could he think about playing at a time like this? He had no idea where Gramps's things were, and Zack could be anywhere—though the further he went the more likely Zack would be behind him!

At this realization, Jeremy's shoulders hunched and his head tried to pull down between them, like an alarmed turtle's.

From his right, in the next row, came a scratching sound. Jeremy froze. He hid behind the end of the rack of shelves and snuck a quick glance around the corner. As far as he could see, there was nothing. Scratch, scratch, SCRATCH, again, right by his side!

139

Two green eyes stared up at him. Curled peacefully on a box, Cleopatra yawned.

"Cleo!" Jeremy whispered, clapping his hand over his mouth to keep from shrieking with surprise and delight.

"Think, don't talk," sounded Cleo's voice in his mind.

"You can't be here!" Jeremy thought loudly. "It's impossible!"

Cleo sat up straight, swished her tail impatiently, and looked at Jeremy as if he were a foolish kitten. "Silly boy," her voice purred in his mind. "Ar-r-ren't you happy to see me? Shall I arrange to disappear-r-r?"

"No!" Jeremy thought, nearly yelling out loud as Cleo got to her feet. "Stay, please! It's just that you almost scared me to death!"

"Well, well. We are nervous, aren't we! But *I'm* not the one who wants to scare you to death. He's out there somewhere."

"Who . . . what?" Jeremy stammered mentally, "I mean, *how* did you get here and how did you get *inside*?"

"Oh, that! These old buildings have all kinds of holes. The mice use them, so why shouldn't I? But we'd better get moving. I smell those nasty Spawn around, and they mean business."

Cleopatra cocked her head and listened, her whiskers twitching.

"Cleo," Jeremy thought, "how can we find the *Shaiféir al Shehn*? There's so much stuff in here we'll never get through it all!"

The cat's green-gold eyes narrowed and a sound very much like laughter rippled through Jeremy's mind.

"How *do* you humans survive with so little talent!" she purred. "I was just a kitten when we went to your grandfather's apartment, but I remember how that book smelled. Just like a human—so busy *seeing*, you never bother to sniff. I suppose I'll have to do ever-r-rything, as usual."

140

Footsteps echoed from the far end of the room. Cleo jumped from the box and padded quickly down the aisle. Jeremy followed her upraised tail as if he were tied to it.

Up and down they went, in and out of the rows of shelves. Jeremy waited uneasily when Cleo stopped to sniff at boxes, and scooted after when she trotted on. Sharing her mind, he smelled everything she did: spice and fragrant oils, dusty cloth and perfumes, moldy books and floor wax, muddy statues and bird feathers, mouse droppings and paint, grease and old newsprint, leather and wood.

Jeremy's mind swam with scents he'd never noticed before, and his nose twitched. At last, Cleo stood still, tail up with its tip twitching sharply side to side, nose sniffing in every direction.

"Hr-r-rmm," she thought, curling her lips in a satisfied smile. "A lot to smell and something to tell."

She turned down an aisle that for some reason was twice as wide as the others. On both sides, the shelves ran right up to the back wall.

A faint odor teased Jeremy's mind: the musty, spicy scent of pipe tobacco. Tears welled in his eyes as he remembered sitting next to Grandpa Heinrich while he puffed out fragrant clouds of smoke.

Cleopatra jumped onto a large box on the lowest shelf and stretched to sniff carefully at a smaller box just above Jeremy's head. There was no mistaking the pungent odor of Gramps's Turkish tobacco. Scrawled on the box with a heavy black marker pen were the words

HELLER—NEAR EAST—BOOKS

Cleo jumped down, wrapped herself in her tail, and smiled as if she'd just finished a can of tuna and was expecting another.

Jeremy hoisted the heavy box onto his shoulder and lowered it carefully to the floor, grunting with effort. He ripped

141

off the tape, tore open the flaps, and began to lift out books, cringing at the noise but too excited to slow down.

Toward the bottom, he hauled out a heavy, leather-bound book covered with beautiful golden designs. "The *Shaiféir al Shehn*, Cleo," he whispered. "This is it."

The light switch clicked and the room went black. Sounds of footsteps approached from the far end of the basement, as someone, or some *thing*, steadily stalked closer. "Oh, oh," Cleopatra thought. "Now I understand how the mice feel. If only you humans knew how to do things quietly, we might not be in this hole."

As Jeremy's sight adjusted to the darkness, he could make out the green glint of Cleo's eyes. He knew she saw far more than he did, for cats see as well in the dark as humans do in daylight. What she saw now was the most frightened human she could imagine.

"I've got to be able to see the book," Jeremy thought desperately. "Whatever we need to do to stop *Ordúrrg-Zaikh*, it's in here." He turned the pages blindly, putting his nose right up to the print. "It's no use, I can't see a thing."

Cleopatra padded up onto his knee and stared at the book. "I can see it," she said.

"What good is that if you can't read," Jeremy said.

"*You* can read, silly boy, through *my* eyes."

The footsteps were sounding closer and closer, but Jeremy blocked out his panic and concentrated on Cleo's mind.

"I can see better," he thought, "but something's wrong. It doesn't make sense. Oh no!" he wailed inwardly, staring at the strange, graceful writing "It's in Primal Script. No way can I read this!"

"Maybe whatever is shining in your pocket would help," the cat suggested calmly.

"The ankh!" Jeremy thought, reaching for the stone and placing it on the book. "I forgot all about it."

Now he could see Cleo, who changed color in the shimmering crystal light as if she were sitting beneath a neon sign. He focused on her mind until he could make out the writing word by word, and as he did this, the ink appeared to flow, re-forming into English.

"King Solomon," he read slowly, "learned from the great Queen of Sheba the mysteries of Egypt. Mightiest among them was the Spell of Isis, the *Caern Isaeth*, for it could banish demons and sweep their evil from the Earth."

In the darkness at the head of their row, the footsteps came to a stop. Behind them was the wall; on both sides, packed shelves; and in front, Zack—or something worse.

There was a slow, dragging sound, as if something was intently crawling toward them.

"Zack?" Jeremy yelled, coughing as his breath caught in his throat.

"Zack?" Cleo thought curiously.

"Zack!" a deep, harsh voice echoed in the darkness.

For a moment, there was silence, a huge, hostile silence in which Jeremy heard his heart beating wildly. Then, a match was struck, and its flare framed Zack. He was crouching, holding the match in one hand and a small leather flask in the other. On the floor was a mixed pile of blue and yellow powders.

Zack looked up at Jeremy and grinned, the flame of the match reflecting in his glasses. "I got this stuff when little Jeremy was shopping for a present for his mommy," Zack mocked, pouring the liquid onto the powder. "That old bastard MacIvery wouldn't sell it, so I took it."

"He wouldn't sell it because it's dangerous," Jeremy said. "Don't light it, Zack! There's no telling what could happen! Give me the matches."

"Give me that book," Zack challenged, "and you can have the matches, and the powder too."

"No!" Jeremy yelled, clutching the book. "It's mine. It was my grandpa's, and now it's mine!"

Zack's scornful laughter echoed in the room. He dropped the burning match into the powders and stepped aside.

For a moment, Zack was swallowed by darkness. Then the powders burst into a red pillar of flame stretching from floor to ceiling.

Dazzled, Jeremy flung up his arms to cover his eyes, dropping the book and the ankh. He staggered back against the wall.

"You never know what dreams—or nightmares—might get loose," Mr. MacIvery had said about the powders.

Now, squinting through a crack between his arms, Jeremy saw a nightmare. Grinning straight at him, Zack stepped into the flame.

"No," Jeremy screamed, "Zack! Stop!" Then his mouth fell open in amazement. In the midst of the flame, Zack stood unhurt.

The fire began to spin, slowly at first and then faster and faster, like a small tornado, turning deeper and deeper red until Zack was hidden. Then the column of flame flowed and shaped itself, rising and twisting to the height of the shelf tops.

From there, as the fire turned solid like glowing volcanic magma cooling into rock, the huge red eye of *Ordúrrg-Zaikh* stared down, flooding the darkness with its glare.

19 TENNIS, ANYONE?

The Dragon stalked forward, its roar exploding into caustic laughter. The floor rocked with each movement and the air trembled. Jeremy's throat burned with the ammonia breath of the great beast. On each of its shining white teeth, through the red-tinged light, he saw his own face reflected.

A giant claw reached down slowly, not for Jeremy but for something on the floor in front of him. "Cleo!" he shouted, "watch out! It's after the *Shaiféir al Shehn*!"

Cleopatra darted from beneath the shelves and crouched in front of *Ordúrrg-Zaikh*, snarling and spitting like a wildcat. The huge creature hesitated just long enough for Jeremy to dash forward and scoop up the book and the ankh. Then the Dragon moved.

As its massive tail whistled past, a great wind flung Jeremy back against the wall. Cleo leapt for the shelves with a wild yowl, trying to stay ahead of the surging tail, but it caught up to her in mid-air and smashed her like a bat crushing a softball. There was a sickening crunch, and she flew across the aisle and crashed in a jumble of falling boxes.

"Cleo!" Jeremy screamed, scrambling toward her. But the monstrous tail coiled and uncoiled again, whipping across the aisle. Jeremy dropped and rolled to the wall, the wind lashing at his hair and clothes. "Oh, Cleo!" he sobbed, "I'm so sorry. Please don't die."

The floor quaked as the monstrous reptile strode forward. Jeremy opened the *Shaiféir al Shehn*, but he was sobbing so hard that it slipped from his hands again. The beast bent toward him, its laughter swelling in the room. Like an inflamed

145

sore, the huge red eye descended, while Jeremy clutched the book and curled against the wall.

From the start of this adventure, Jeremy had felt pulled in two directions, backward and forward. All his doubts about his own courage and goodness dragged him back, while his love for Sara and his family and friends pulled him forward.

Jeremy was the monkey in the middle of a wild tug of war, as if tied to thick braided ropes yanked ever harder by these negative and positive forces. If the positive rope broke, he would give up in defeat and *Ordúrrg-Zaikh* would win the world.

But because of Jeremy's many small acts of courage since he'd first set out with Alaikin, the negative rope had worn thin, its braids parting one by one. Now, with the shock of losing Cleo, he felt the last strand of doubt snap, and was shot forward by a powerful new belief in himself. Defiance erupted within him, righteous rage against the Dragon.

Rolling away from the wall, he sprang to his feet and screamed into the massive snout of *Ordúrrg-Zaikh*, "You'll have to kill me to get this book!" The words tore from his throat like a tiger's roar. "You'll have to kill me right now!"

At that moment, he was icy calm, as if, by risking death itself to save those he loved, he had redeemed all his past failures and become invincible. It was the first time in his life he had ever felt this way, and it was wonderful, but didn't last long. As the mocking laughter of *Ordúrrg-Zaikh* slowly died away and it's unblinking eye fixed on him, his knees began to tremble.

What have I done, his panicked thoughts squeaked, while his hard-won calm cracked like river ice in Spring. Everything went quiet, as in the eye of a hurricane, except for the beast's bellows breath and his own tiny panting.

Jeremy waited, his stomach now fluttering along with his knees. There was nowhere to run, nothing to do but stand and fight, even if the murderous teeth slashed him to bits. Yet the parted jaws came no closer, and the tail when it moved did so slowly. Uncoiling like an enormous python, it snaked forward until its tip rose from the floor and wound around Jeremy's waist—an icy, numbing lariat. Then the tail pulled him slowly forward, closer and closer to the horrific body.

Jeremy's gaze traveled along the massive feet, gripping like twisted roots, up the huge legs and bulging trunk, past the T-Rex sized teeth, and stopped finally at the bloated eye that glared down from high above. The poisonous stench of the creature's breath washed over him. He gagged until his knees began to buckle and he felt, strangely, that he might fall *upward* and drown in that infected red pool of an eye.

The voice of *Ordúrrg-Zaikh* rumbled like a rocket launch. "So, Guardian, you think you can command me? You say I must kill you *now*? Oh no, Earth-born. I kill when I please, not on your orders."

Remembering the calm he'd felt moments ago somehow gave Jeremy the strength to collect himself again. He clenched every muscle to stop his body from shaking, and made a brain-splitting effort to think.

"How do you know I am a *Ouyperkai*?" he choked out, swaying on his feet but standing straight and tall.

Ordúrrg-Zaikh sensed some change in its adversary, a new edge that made it pause. The huge Dragon cocked its head and studied him.

"Come, Earth-born," it warned at last, "no tricks." Jeremy recognized a new tone, one of reluctant respect.

It's worried about me, he thought in amazement. It could stomp me like a worm, but it's worried. Then he had an inspiration: a way to gain time to work out some plan. Knowing that *Ordúrrg-Zaikh* could read his strongest thoughts, he would hide them by playing a tennis match in his mind.

Jeremy imagined a player to stand in for him, like an avatar in a video game. Tall and muscular, his avatar stretched high to power a serve. Then he needed to create another avatar, of *Ordúrrg-Zaikh* itself, to receive the serve, so he imagined a mini-dragon and placed it on his mental court. He held down a smile as his mind's eye gazed with satisfaction at the puny creature he'd created. This mental video game would hide his thoughts and his real intentions, Jeremy hoped—if the Dragon did not see through it.

"We have met once before, through the lens of the Flowering Crystal," the great beast rumbled, glaring at Jeremy suspiciously. "My memory is as long as my power is great."

Jeremy's avatar served, and the game began. "You're pretty big all right," he flattered the monster, sensing weakness behind its boasting, "but the dragon I saw in the *Zhystrém Haistrál* was even bigger. Don't tell me you've shrunk!" His voice quaked, but for his plan to succeed he needed not only to flatter the creature but also to goad and risk offending it.

"Shrunk!" the beast shrieked, its forked tongue flicking between rows of dagger teeth. "Impudent Earth-dung! You met *Ordúrrg-Zaikh*, the Great Dragon, who I assure you has not shrunk. I am *Zaikh-Ka*, reflection of that awesome might, an emanation to carry out its will while it rests in the Dark Shrine. But be warned, the Great Dragon powers me and every emanation, for we *are Ordúrrg-Zaikh* in all but size."

In Jeremy's mind game, the mini-Dragon swung its racquet with its tail and a shot flew back at him. The real *Zaikh-Ka* paused, tilted its head, and appraised him.

"You are very fond of this Earth game of tennis, *Ouyper-kai*, to think of it now."

"My dad played in college," Jeremy replied, "and we practice together. I love my dad and he loves me, so when I'm scared, thinking about tennis makes me feel better."

Zaikh-Ka looked pleased. "You are wise to be frightened of me," it boasted. "I killed your grandfather, and I can kill you *and* your father any time I care to."

It's working, Jeremy thought as he made his avatar smash a return shot. Blinded by vanity, the Dragon had bought his tennis story, so he had at least a chance of thinking up a plan undetected, screened by his imaginary game.

"How did you get here," Jeremy asked, breathing more evenly now, "and what did you do with Zack?"

"My flesh feeds on the energy of the Earth-child who serves me, and so I live and grow."

"Then without Zack to serve you," Jeremy replied, "without his energy, you couldn't be here at all!"

"Clever, Earth-born," snarled *Zaikh-Ka*, with a low rumble that had to pass for a chuckle. "Worthy of a *Brỹle-Ouyperkai*. So you know why I would rather win you over than kill you."

"Yes," Jeremy answered, the start of a plan itching in his mind—a terribly risky plan, but the only one he could think of. "Then you could feed on my energy and grow even bigger. But if you kill me, no more energy, and you're on a diet."

"Think, Earth-child," roared *Zaikh-Ka*. "Imagine what I can offer! Once before, you tasted my power, and like a fool you refused me. But then you were safe behind the Crystal lens, and your life was not in question. Now, think again of what you could gain—or lose."

"I get to live if I live for you, is that it?" Jeremy asked.

"Well said, Earth-child. That *is* it precisely."

"What do I have to do?"

"Just give me that book," *Zaikh-Ka* said in a potent whisper, rolling its great eye and caressing its teeth with flickering tongue. "Give me the *Shaiféir al Shehn* of your own free will. Thus will you join me and leave your foolish Earth-mind."

"Is that all?" Jeremy replied. "That's easy. I never wanted that crummy book anyway. But wait! What do I get for it?"

"Anything. Anything you desire."

"All right," Jeremy said loudly, forcing himself to step toward *Zaikh-Ka* as his avatar hit an overhead smash to disguise his elation. "It's a deal—if you give me the same power you have. I never wanted to be a *Ouyperkai* in the first place. They tricked me into it because they couldn't find anybody else."

20 THE BATTLE LOST AND WON

"The *Shaiféir al Shehn*," the Dragon hissed impatiently, spreading its claws and coiling its tail. "Give me the book!"

"Whoa, wait just a minute!" Jeremy exclaimed, coughing and covering his face to fend off the fumes. "Before I give you the *Shaiféir al Shehn*, I want to check out this power you're supposed to give me. You know what you're going to get, so it's only fair that I see what I'll get."

Please, Jeremy prayed to himself, fall for it!—but he showed nothing on his face as his avatar returned the mini-dragon's sideline shot. He had to hide his hopes, but he didn't and couldn't hide the fear and pleading that crept into his voice. Just as well—the beast had to believe he was afraid or it would know something was up.

The huge eye rolled suspiciously and the tail lashed sullenly from side to side. "Don't bother me with *fair*," bellowed *Zaikh-Ka*. "I have no use for *fair*. Give me the book, Earth-scum! Then you'll get what's coming to you."

"I don't like the sound of that," Jeremy yelled into the Dragon's teeth. "No deal!" He ran back to the wall and huddled over the *Shaiféir al Shehn*. Then he took a deep breath and dared the scariest step in his secret plan. He would defeat the Dragon with its own weaknesses—greed and vanity.

"I said you'd have to kill me, and I wasn't kidding. Too bad if you lose all that yummy energy!"

"You dare to taunt me!" roared *Zaikh-Ka*, shaking its huge head and gnashing its teeth. Its tail snapped through the air like an enormous bullwhip and smashed into the wall inches above Jeremy's head. The whole building shook.

"Your energy means no more to me than that of an earthworm. You think you are *Ouyperkai*, and that will protect you?" the great beast sneered. "Now hear the truth! I killed your grandfather and you have not a fraction of his power. You are a failure, a coward who could not save anyone, even those closest to you. You are not worthy to join me. Be grateful that I take pity on you, worm, and do not pulp you as you stand."

The Dragon lifted one immense hind leg and squeezed its long toes into a clawed fist not a foot from Jeremy's face, all the time glaring down at him.

Zaikh-Ka was right, Jeremy realized with a black lurch of his guts. The beast might be vain, but it was oh so cunning. It had played along with him, made him think he was winning. Then it had turned the tables and found *his* weakness—not the obvious physical one but his deeper failure of character— and now the game was lost.

Zack, his best friend, had been taken over by *Zaikhthréem* and his energy fed to the hungry darkness because Jeremy was not smart or brave enough to help him. Sara was sliding into madness, and now he had gotten Cleo killed helping him because he couldn't help himself.

Everything was his fault. The Dragon was right, he was worthless. Any remnant of the strength he had briefly felt now melted away. Jeremy was spinning down into darkness, a small, shrieking whirlwind of grief. Even Alaikin had abandoned him, and rightly so.

"Yes, believe it," the beast crooned in the pleasure of its triumph, "you are even worse than I have said. Your tennis match is over and you have lost. A pity! I was starting to enjoy it." The Dragon distilled its malice into a low, hoarse laugh that Jeremy felt flow over him like a wave of slime.

"Enough wasting time, Earth-scum," the huge creature rumbled. "Give me the *Shaiféir al Shehn*!"

Zaikh-Ka was clever enough to use Jeremy's self-doubt against him, but not smart enough to refrain from celebrating. It was the beast's laughter at its presumed triumph that freed Jeremy from his downward spiral. That and a shaft of golden light that shot across his dark free-fall and opened like a saving parachute within his mind and heart.

"Stuff and nonsense, all of it," twanged the familiar voice, "you know that. Don't swoon for lizard tricks. Too much at stake for self-pity."

And Jeremy knew that he had nearly fallen for the Dragon's most devious ploy—using his own lack of confidence to break him down so he would give away the book, and himself, out of despair. All because of the delusion, planted and nurtured by his adversary, that he himself was to blame for everything that had gone wrong.

Now Jeremy saw clearly where the evil lay, and it was not in him. And now he saw where the weakness truly was. Not in him. He had not lost, not yet, and with *Zaikh-Ka* now off guard and sure of victory, he had his best shot to take.

"Okay, okay," Jeremy yelled, squeezing down into the crease where the wall met the floor as if to ooze through a crack. "I'm sorry I resisted you. I was a fool to think I was anything but a weak little nothing, and you showed me the truth. I yield to your great power."

His avatar's volley caught the tape and hung atop the net, spinning, neither falling back nor trickling over.

"It's just that we Earth-types, even if we don't deserve it, like things to be fair. I'm just a worm's worth of energy for you, but if I give you *The Book of Life* of my own free will, shouldn't I get some idea of what I'll get for that? I'm only asking for a preview. You mean to tell me that with all your power you won't let me try some for one little minute?"

Zaikh-Ka cocked its gigantic head to one side, as if thinking intensely, weighing certain gain against some distant consequence it couldn't imagine. The power of the *Shaiféir al Shehn* would be greater if freely given, not taken by force, and after all, what threat could this trivial Earth-creature possibly represent?

Stomach knotted, Jeremy tried to look tiny and harmless, as if he would never, ever, dream of challenging so mighty a creature as *Zaikh-Ka*. The Dragon measured him with slightly parted jaws, tongue caressing the tips of its teeth—its version, Jeremy thought, of a furrowed brow. Silence. The ball spun atop the net. Which way would it fall?

Zaikh-Ka returned its head to the vertical, opened its mouth further, and with a sharp jerk inclined it toward Jeremy. He flinched, expecting to be skewered. "Very well then," thundered the beast, nodding slightly and somehow managing to look pleased. "I accept your apology, and your praise."

The avatar's shot dropped on the mini-dragon's side of the net. This could do it, Jeremy thought, choking back his excitement—game, set, maybe match. "You may taste the greatness of my power," *Zaikh-Ka* said intensely, "but then you will return that power to me *and* give me the *Shaiféir al Shehn*. Be sure to keep your promise, Earth-dung. I am not kind to those who would trick me."

Once more the huge tail whistled over Jeremy's head and the roar echoed from the walls. Then the swollen, flame-red eye moved lower and lower, closer and closer, until it forced him nearly to the floor. Trapped, he started to panic, wondering if *Zaikh-Ka* meant to crush him, deal or not.

Fiery light flooded over him, soaking through his skin as through paper. He felt flushed and swollen, as if he'd spent too long beside a roaring fire or was running a high fever. In a second, the red light welled up inside his body, surged through his limbs and glared in his brain. A ruby mist glazed his eyes, and his bones and muscles began to crack and bulge. His heart pounded against his chest like a wrecking ball, driving rivers of blood with each tremendous beat.

Jeremy could only hope that he would somehow manage to turn the Dragon power surging through him in the direction he'd planned: against *Zaikh-Ka* itself. He knew that he would fall under the giant reptile's spell, just as Zack had, unless he could resist the temptation to use the power selfishly. What he didn't know was *how* he could resist.

The floor fell away as Jeremy grew, his flesh straining like a mutant plant reaching toward the boiling, blood-colored sun of the Dragon's giant eye. As his body swelled, so did a riot of hatred within him, the huge rage he'd felt in the cave of the *Ordúrrg-Zaikh.*

Reeling with crazy dreams of destruction, Jeremy reared up beside *Zaikh-Ka* and screamed a wild laugh of triumph. He would rule the world and crush anybody who got in his way: teachers, parents, everyone. Nothing could stop him. Nobody would ever touch him again. Just as in the Great Dragon's cave, the gloating voice of the *Zaikh-Ka* boomed.

"Who would oppose me, when I offer eternal triumph?"

But even as the massive creature's violence exploded through Jeremy's body, the words of the *Zhystrém Haistrál* whispered in his mind. "Without love, the greatest power leads only to destruction." Suddenly, as if he was drowning, memories of everyone important to him passed before his eyes.

"Help me," Sara pleaded, as the *Zaikthréem* boiled around her.

"We love you, Jerry," cried his mother and father.

"Charley boy," Zack crooned, with the goofy smile *Ordúrrg-Zaikh* had taken from him, and he joined Sandy in petting the old dog.

"Cheerio, old top," said Alaikin, as the *melis* tumbled in the meadow and Cleo yawned sleepily.

"Cleo," Jeremy murmured sadly—but Cleo had just been killed by the very Dragon that promised him eternal triumph. In that instant, he knew that the boasting of *Zaikh-Ka* was hollow. The Dragon offered not eternal triumph, but eternal betrayal. Jeremy's rage remained as enormous as his body had grown, but turned now against a new target. It was *Zaikh-Ka* he wanted to crush, and he had grown to nearly its size.

With a gigantic scream, he threw himself on the monster. He gripped its jaws and twisted its head back with all the strength it had given him. *Zaikh-Ka* fought savagely, flexing its great tail overhead and wrapping it around Jeremy's neck. They swayed together, locked equally in each other's power, Horus and Seth in battle again.

Then the Dragon's powerful tail slowly forced Jeremy's giant, hawk-headed body back, until he was in the same position Horus had been during the struggle in the tomb. Just as Jeremy thought he would break in half, *Zaikh-Ka* shook its jaws free of his grip and roared out its rage.

"By *Ordúrrg-Zaikh*, the Great Dragon, I withdraw the power betrayed. This *Ouyperkai* must die."

With a wrench of its enormous tail, *Zaikh-Ka* flung Jeremy down. His falling body brushed and rocked the racks of shelves that in turn hailed down boxes and packages. Jeremy felt as if a plug had been pulled from his body, letting all of his blood drain out. He seemed to fall and fall, as in a nightmare, through miles of distance and hours of time. He shrank smaller and smaller, like a deflating balloon zooming around a kid's birthday party.

At last, he found himself huddled against the wall, a little kid again, trapped beneath the blood-red eye. Was the power ever really his, or had he merely been hypnotized by *Zaikh-Ka*? What did it matter? Either way, his brief spell as a giant was like the memory of a long-ago dream. He had just one chance left now, and that was the *Caern Isaeth*.

As the Dragon moved in, Jeremy grabbed the *Shaiféir al Shehn* from the floor and searched wildly through the pages. When the beast's breath touched him, he looked up and saw again, reflected in its huge teeth, a whole row of Jeremys, each crouching helplessly over the book.

"It's no use," he screamed, and the Jeremys echoed. "I can't read the Spell."

Zaikh-Ka threw back its head, and its laugh boomed like thunder in a ravine as it took a moment to gloat. "Yes, Earth-scum, too late. Think of what you might have had if you had not betrayed me. Think of this as I grind you between my teeth."

But Jeremy hardly heard, for he was listening to another voice, a small voice that sang only in his mind, piercing the Dragon's rumbling like a clear silver bell.

"First I will show, and then you will know."

"Help me, Alaikin!" Jeremy shouted. "I can't read the *Shaiféir al Shehn*!"

"The ankh can read it, Jeremy. Remember, the ankh is the eye of the *Zhystrém Haistrál.*"

"What is this?" rumbled the Dragon, its laughter fading to an uneasy chuckle as Jeremy stood frozen. "Another Earth-dung trick?" Rolling its eye and swiveling its huge head, the monster searched the room.

Jeremy saw his chance, darted forward, and scooped the ankh from the floor.

"Aha!" roared *Zaikh-Ka*, turning its attention back to its victim. "Tricks and spells won't help you now, Earth-slime. Now, you die."

Dragon fumes rolled over Jeremy, and a wave of blackness washed through his head. He staggered and leaned back against the wall, clutching the ankh with all his strength—but the *Shaiféir al Shehn* grew too heavy and toppled to the floor. Jeremy's legs buckled and he pitched forward onto his hands and knees. In darkness dense as mud over a grave he felt around the floor until his hand found the book.

"For Sara and Mom and Dad and Cleo and everybody!" he muttered, as the red light of *Zaikh-Ka* pierced the fog of its fumes and its jaws reached for him. With a desperate lunge, he slapped the ankh on the *Shaiféir al Shehn*.

The vast jaws of *Zaikh-Ka* froze in mid-bite. The colors of the ankh pulsed brighter and brighter, flooding the whole room with deep, radiant light, and the chiming voice of the *Zhystrém Haistrál* began to sing the rhymes of the *Caern Isaeth*, the great spell of the goddess Isis.

The battle for worlds,
Forever begun,
Can never be lost,
And never won.

Dragon be gone,
With Horus and Seth.
Life be life,
Death be death.

Only the Balance
Is blessed.
Only the Balance
Is blessed.

With the last words of the spell, the red light began to fade from the Dragon's eye, and the blackness drained from Jeremy's mind. He saw the giant reptile shudder and sway as its strength melted.

Falling, it grabbed at the shelves on both sides. The huge racks rocked violently, smashing against each other. Then *Zaikh-Ka* lost its grip and plunged backward in a storm of boxes.

Just before a large, heavy package hit Jeremy on the back of the head, he saw the fallen monster shimmer like a mirage and dissolve into the fire from which it had come. By the time that pillar of flame had burned down to a heap of gray ash, Jeremy was unconscious.

Next to the ashes lay Zack, as if asleep. A gentle smile curved his lips, as if he was having a lovely dream.

21 A WHACKING GREAT STORY

"Well, lad," said Mr. MacIvery as Jeremy opened his eyes. "It's about time you came to. You've been in dreamland nearly two hours."

Jeremy seemed to be gazing through a dirty veil. He sensed that something had gone badly wrong, though he didn't yet know what. He had no idea how he'd come to be lying in a bed with hospital equipment all around and he didn't recognize the old man gazing down at him with a kindly, concerned expression. I must have really screwed up this time, he thought dismally.

"Where am I?" he asked, wincing as a dull pain thudded in his head.

"In County Hospital," Mr. MacIvery answered. "You had a pretty nasty knock."

"How did I get hurt?" Jeremy asked, bewildered. "What are you doing here?"

"Do you not remember anything?" the Scotsman questioned sharply. "Nothing at all?" he continued in a softer, coaxing tone.

Jeremy shook his head and then regretted it, as the pain in his skull pounded.

"You'd better not move," the old shopkeeper sighed. "I promised the nurse to keep you quiet. But you really don't recall what happened at the Museum? You and Zack left quite a mess."

"Zack?" Jeremy asked, thinking hard, even though it made him wince. "The Museum? Wait a minute. You're Mr. MacIvery, right? We visited you in your shop, and you had those

158

magic powders. I do remember something . . . Wow, I remember a lot!"

"Well, you may want to tell me sometime, though don't strain yourself now—nurse's orders. But I am thankful somebody remembers, because Zack claims he doesn't. Not even how he got there."

"Where is Zack?" Jeremy said quickly, raising his head and then letting it down as softly as he could when pain knifed his skull. "Is he okay?"

"Calm down," Mr. MacIvery said, laying a leathery hand gently on Jeremy's forehead. "Excitement's no good for concussion, and that's what the medicos say you've got. Zack is in better shape than you, except that he can't remember a thing about this evening, to save his life."

"Are my mom and dad coming?" Jeremy asked, half dreading the answer.

"Of course," the old man said. "The hospital phoned them."

"Mr. MacIvery," Jeremy asked solemnly, "how am I going to explain it to them?"

"Explain what?" the Scotsman replied with an amused smile, lifting his bushy eyebrows.

Tears welled in Jeremy's eyes, and though he fought them back, they began to trickle down his cheeks. "What will I tell them about the Museum," he sniffed, "and missing Mom's special dinner, and everything . . ."

"Calm yourself, Jeremy," Mr. MacIvery said. He pulled a huge, wrinkled handkerchief from his coat pocket and wiped Jeremy's wet face. "You have nothing to explain as far as the Museum's concerned. Missing your mother's dinner, now that's more serious."

"You're teasing me," Jeremy said, fresh tears oozing out between his eyelids the more he squeezed them shut. "That's not nice."

"Tut, tut," the old Scotsman said in exasperation, "no more tears, eh? Listen, and I'll explain. It's very simple."

"Well?" Jeremy demanded, fending off Mr. MacIvery's musty, stained handkerchief and wiping his face with the bed sheet.

"After you left the shop," the old man began, crumpling the offending object and stuffing it back into his coat pocket, "I spent the rest of the day wondering. You were very eager to get that book, and your young friend Zack even more so.

"I didna like what I saw of Zack, I must tell you. A rough-seeming fellow, and when I discovered at closing time that my powders were missing, it was short work to guess who had them."

"Yes, he took them," Jeremy said. "I'm sorry, Mr. MacIvery, I didn't know."

"I'm sure you didn't, lad. But I knew that the powders would be very dangerous in his hands—and I expect you know that too, now."

"Yes," said Jeremy, shrinking back under the shopkeeper's keen glance.

"Well," Mr. MacIvery continued, "any fool could tell that trouble was brewing, and this fool could guess where it would boil over. It was after five o'clock, but I happen to be a friend of Mr. Carswell, the Museum's Assistant Director, and he gave me the guard's phone number at home. When the guard told me that you two had gone in but he hadn't seen you come out—well, that clinched it."

"He went back to the Museum and let you in?" Jeremy questioned.

"Right you are, lad. And we found you knocked cold and Zack dreaming like a baby and an unholy mess of shelves and boxes everywhere."

"That's what I mean," Jeremy nearly shouted. "What am I going to tell Mom and Dad about all that?"

"About what?" the old man said again, his eyes twinkling. "Nothing was broken, Jeremy. The shelves can be put back and the boxes stacked upon them. That will take but a few hours for the guard and me, while the Museum's closed tomorrow. And the poor man is overjoyed at the monetary reward his labor will bring him, so long as he forgets to mention it to anyone!"

"Mr. MacIvery," Jeremy grinned, "you're a wonderful man." The Scotsman smiled and bowed, but Jeremy's grin faded. "How am I going to explain being here, with this?" Jeremy wailed. He touched the bump on the back of his head and flinched.

"You'll use your imagination," Mr. MacIvery said, grinning. "You're getting pretty good at that lately, from what I can deduce. Perhaps a dragon smacked you with its tail?"

"What?" Jeremy asked, his eyes wide with astonishment, "you know everything, then?"

"No, Jeremy," the old man answered. "I don't know *everything*, but I do know a great deal, and I can take a good guess at the rest. It makes a whacking great story, doesn't it?"

The nurse bustled into the room. "Jeremy!" she exclaimed cheerily, "how nice to see you awake, and just in time for your parents. They'll be here any minute, to see you before you go to X-ray."

"I'll get out of your way," Mr. MacIvery said to the nurse.

"Oh, but you're not at all in the way," she replied, "and I'm sure his parents will want to thank you."

"No," the Scotsman said quickly, cringing. "No thanks necessary. Anyone would have helped. Goodbye," he continued, grasping Jeremy's hand quickly and turning away.

"Wait," Jeremy yelled as the old man made for the door. "What about Cleo?"

"Cleo?" Mr. MacIvery asked, turning back. "Who's Cleo?"

"My cat—Cleopatra. She was in the . . . she was there!"

"I'm sorry, Jeremy, but I saw no cat. Are you sure she was there?"

"Yes, I'm sure," Jeremy said glumly. "Goodbye. And thank you for everything."

"Ta ta," the old man said. "Come see me at the shop when you're feeling better."

If Cleo's body wasn't there, she must have survived and got away, Jeremy thought with growing excitement. Maybe she would be waiting for him at home. Unless she was mortally wounded and had crawled off to die in private, as animals do.

"Cleo," Jeremy murmured, tears welling up again. "You *have* to be okay!"

"Jeremy," the nurse asked, stroking his forehead, "shall I get you something for the pain?"

"No," he moaned. "It won't help."

Jeremy's hope again gave way to despair. Now he was certain that Cleo was dead and buried out of sight under a pile of boxes. That was why Mr. MacIvery had missed her. "She was so smart," he thought, stifling a sob, "finding the *Shaiféir al Shehn* and then showing me how to read it. And so brave, a tiny cat taking on *Ordúrrg-Zaikh* without a second thought."

Then Jeremy remembered how he'd felt after the monster smashed Cleo with its horrible tail. He was completely calm and in control, as if he could not fail, would never fail at anything again. He'd focused all his energy and invention on finding a way to stop the huge beast, and knew he would give that task the best he had, no matter what happened. He'd become fearless, like Cleo, and clever too, as never before.

Had he learned that from her, perhaps even "caught it" from her when they were mind sharing? Backed up against a wall, with no way out but forward, they'd stood together for what they believed in and those they loved.

If she really is gone, Jeremy thought, at least I can remember her by the courage she gave me. No more chickening out and screwing up—I swear to be as brave and smart as she was. He pulled himself up straighter in bed, ignoring the throbbing of his head. Even if I have to fight ten dragons.

At that moment his mother rushed into the room and started toward him, arms wide. "Hi Mom," he said quickly and cheerfully, as if he hadn't a care in the world. "I'm sorry I missed your special dinner."

"Jerry!" she exclaimed, biting her lip and stopping with her hands hovering above him, as if afraid to touch him. "Who cares about the dinner! I just want to know that you're alright!" When Jeremy winced as he nodded, she still held back, as if she didn't believe him.

"He's doing fine now," the nurse said lightly. "Don't worry."

Then Jeremy's mother caressed his cheek and bent to kiss him. "Mo-o-m!" he protested, squirming a bit, "it's no big deal, just a concussion."

His mother straightened up, brushed tears from her cheeks, and planted her hands on her hips. "Jeremy," she said with exasperation, "I swear if you hadn't already hurt yourself I'd strangle you. After everything that's happened to us, you turn up with a broken skull and say it's no big deal?"

"The boy does have some explaining to do," Jeremy's father said as he came into the room. He walked to the bed, put his hand on Jeremy's shoulder, and looked at him sternly.

Oh, oh, Jeremy thought, squeezing his eyes closed. Here's where I'm going to get it!

But his dad said nothing more, and when Jeremy opened his eyes again he was amazed to see him grin and wink slyly.

"You actually look pretty good for somebody who took such a bad knock," he said, squeezing Jeremy's shoulder and then turning to smile reassuringly at his wife.

Good old Dad, Jeremy thought. His father seemed to be welcoming him into a club he hadn't known about before, the world of grown men who can take a hard knock, pick themselves up, and go on.

Dr. Taylor put his arm around this wife. "Jeremy's tough as nails, but let's let him rest for now," he said soothingly, using his best bedside manner on her rather than Jeremy.

Then, when she bristled, he gave her a quick, sharp glance to let her know that he was up to something, and that she should play along. "After all, he's had a pretty bad crack on the noggin, even for a tough guy."

22 ONLY THE BALANCE IS BLESSED

When the x-rays had showed no skull fracture, Jeremy's father had said it was a relief, but then began to look worried. He'd called a neurologist friend and asked him whether they should do an MRI just to be sure there was no bleeding inside the brain. Since the patient showed no sign of confusion or dulled awareness, Dr. Taylor reported, the specialist didn't think more tests were needed.

"We'll bring you home and keep a close eye on you," he continued, "but if you develop any symptoms like those you'll be coming right back for a scan."

So the next morning Jeremy woke up in his own bed. For a few sleepy moments, he thought about what had happened just before they left the hospital.

"I think we can watch him well enough at home," his father had said to the young doctor on duty. "He'll be more comfortable there."

"Just keep him quiet," the doctor replied, wagging his finger at Mrs. Taylor. "He shouldn't get excited, not for a few days."

"Don't worry," Jeremy's father answered, looking away to hide his exasperation with the pushy young physician. "He's in experienced hands."

Now, lying warm beneath his blankets, Jeremy was grateful that nobody seemed to doubt his story about getting the concussion. He'd decided to tell it while he was still sick, just after getting home, so they wouldn't ask many questions, even if they didn't really believe him. He'd managed to fool the Dragon, sort of, but the best story he could come up with sounded weak even to him. Lying to his parents was harder than lying to a monster out to murder him.

"I was running across the street for the bus, so I could get home in time for Mom's dinner," he explained, looking not at them but at the ceiling. "There was some melted ice cream a kid must have dropped, but when I saw it I was already bringing my foot down. I slipped and fell backward and hit my head on the curb.

"It's a good thing Mr. MacIvery was passing on his way home from the Museum—he told me later that he put me in the back of his station wagon and brought me to County Hospital. A lot faster and cheaper than calling an ambulance, he said."

Jeremy held his breath a bit and lightly bit his tongue watching his parents consider his story. They exchanged a quick glance, and he could read both their doubt and their decision not to push him while he was hurt. He might have to come up with something better later, but for now he was off the hook.

Jeremy began to breathe again as his mom spoke. "We will have to thank Mr. MacIvery properly," she said—"I'm sorry he had to rush off before we came, but I suppose he'd already given enough of his time rescuing you.

"That dinner," she continued with an overdramatic grimace, "it caused so much trouble I wish I'd never made it—or burned it."

"No, it was too good to wish for that," his dad replied, smiling. Then his smile pulled down into frown, and he shook his head as he continued. "If I were MacIvery I'd have called an ambulance on finding someone unconscious. The old Scotsman certainly is no medical man. But I suppose you'd expect him to pinch pennies where he can."

He paused, and then his face brightened with a knowing grin. "Someday, maybe, Jeremy will learn not to jaywalk," he said in an exaggerated "father knows best" voice, as if he was fully aware that something was going on but had made a secret pact with Jeremy not to blow his cover.

"Can't the lecture wait until he's better?" his mother retorted a bit sharply, but she was smiling so her husband would know that she knew he was kidding, and Jeremy could tell she was playing along.

* * *

Somebody knocked lightly on Jeremy's door. "Jerry," his mother called softly, "are you awake? I've brought you some breakfast."

"All right, Mom!" Jeremy exclaimed. "I'm hungry."

"Well, you're not supposed to eat a lot today, so you won't get nauseous," his mother said, entering with a breakfast tray. "Just toast and a soft-boiled egg."

"Yuck," Jeremy replied. "Well, okay, as long as the egg's not runny."

"It *was* runny, but I mixed in some concrete to fix that," his mother said, grinning. Jeremy grabbed his throat and made a gagging noise, twisting his face into a poisoned mask. "It's good to see you perking up, Mr. Snip," his mother added with a laugh.

Jeremy relaxed his face and grinned, but then bit his lip anxiously. "Mom, has Cleo come back?" Even though he'd been convinced yesterday evening that Cleo was gone, the bright morning had revived his hope that somehow she'd survived.

"I haven't seen her," his mother answered. "But I wouldn't worry. She's probably off chasing mice."

"Yeah," Jeremy answered, trying to keep smiling for his mother's sake, even as his spirits sank like a brick through water. "You're probably right."

"Jeremy," she said softly, as he forced himself to eat some toast. "Your sister wants to come in and see you. I don't know

166

why, but she's much better this morning—just like her old self."

"Gee Mom," Jeremy said, brightening. I bet I know why, he told himself, but aloud he said only, "that's terrific! Send Sar in as soon as I'm finished with breakfast."

"I called Mr. Tatum last night, after you asked me to. He was sorry to hear you were hurt. Zack and Sandy will come over after school."

"Good," Jeremy answered. "He didn't say anything else, did he? About Zack or anything?"

"What would he say?" she answered, looking at him curiously. "They were having a late dinner so I didn't talk to him long. Oh yes, he did say that Zack looked a little worn out. He thought he might be coming down with something. The flu's early this year."

Zack must really be okay, Jeremy thought, or his dad was too busy to notice if he was still weird. Jeremy imagined Zack—skinny, gawky kid with coke-bottle glasses—goofily jumping up and down, excited about some crazy idea that had just dawned on him. He was happy to think of Zack as a friend once more, instead of the worst enemy he could have. A smile dawned on his face, and spread into a wide grin when, after a brief rustling in the hallway, Sara came in.

"Hi, Freckle-Puss," Jeremy said.

"Hi, Jeremy," she replied, shyly answering his smile. "Mom said you had an accident."

"Yeah," Jeremy answered. "I fell down and got a concussion."

"What's that?" Sara asked. "Can I still get hugs or will I catch it?"

"I banged my head," Jeremy said. "Can you catch that? Come here and I'll give you hugs."

His head hurt as he leaned forward to embrace Sara, but it was worth it. "How are you doing, Sar," he whispered as he clasped his arms around her and rocked her back and forth.

"Okay," she said, "but you're making me dizzy."

"How many freckles do you have now," Jeremy asked, pretending to count them while a knot loosened within him. From the twisted sack of feelings it had tied off came, washing through him like cool, fresh water, the certainty that he really hadn't hurt Sara after all.

"Mom says I have enough freckles for a prize at the fair," Sara said. She put her hand over her mouth to stifle an attack of giggles, and then smiled slyly. "You're gonna have to eat left-overs for a week, Jeremy. Mom said so last night when you missed the stuffed chicken."

"I don't think so, Sar," Jeremy grinned back, taking a deep breath. "Mom found out I couldn't help it."

"Jeremy," Sara said solemnly, "the red wigglers are gone."

"No kidding," Jeremy said. "That's great, Sar! No more red wigglers and lots more freckles."

"Everything's really okay now, huh?"

"Yeah, everything's going to be okay. You haven't seen Cleo, have you?"

"Unh uh," Sara said as Jeremy tousled her hair. "Cleo's a bad cat, she ran away."

"No, Sara," Jeremy said, biting his lip. "Cleo's a great cat. Someday I'll tell you just how wonderful she is."

"Jeremy," his mother said, walking into the room and taking Sara's hand. "I think you should rest now. Your father says you have to take it very easy for a few days, and don't forget Sandy and Zack are coming over later."

"Okay, Mom. I'm sort of sleepy, anyway."

"Good. By the way, Zack called from school. He said he hopes you're feeling better, and to tell you he's sorry. I don't know what he's got to be sorry about, but he said to tell you."

"Gee, Mom, I don't know either," Jeremy said with a huge grin on his face. "Maybe he'll let me know later."

Jeremy's mother gave him a puzzled look, and her hands went to her hips as if he were in for a lecture. But then she shrugged, bent down, and kissed him lightly on the forehead.

It was a good time, he decided, to give her the gift still hidden in his closet.

"Before you go, Mom, I got something for you. I didn't have time to wrap it, but I want to give it to you now, like Mother's Day in advance. Look on the top shelf of my closet, between the sweaters."

"That's very nice of you, Jerry," she said as she opened the closet door and reached for the shelf. "But you really didn't have to."

"I know I didn't," Jeremy replied, "but I wanted to." He watched as she unwrapped the Noh mask, held it, and gazed into its eyes, empty but full of the same calm expressed by the smiling lips and uncreased forehead.

His mother's face softened into an expression like that of the mask itself: peaceful and sweet, as if she had grown younger. This was exactly what he had hoped would happen.

"It's from Mr. MacIvery's shop," he told her. "I thought it might make you happy." Then he waited nervously to see what she would say. She brushed her hand quickly across her eyes, and he wondered if she was crying, and if so, whether it was happy or sad crying.

"Yes, Jerry," she began after a while, "it's made me very happy. It fills me with hope. You have good taste, to find such a lovely thing. I'll have to think of where I want to put it."

She kissed him again on the forehead, rested her hand there for a moment, and then turned to go. "I'll leave the door open a crack," she said, "so you can call me if you need anything."

What more could I need, Jeremy said to himself as he settled back onto his pillow. Sara's rid of the red wigglers, Zack's okay again, Mom's cheering up, and everything's getting better.

As Jeremy began to doze, a warm feeling of pride welled up in his chest. He'd finally gotten something right! But then, as if a black cloud had floated in front of the sun of his happiness, he thought of Cleopatra, and drifted to sleep in deep-ening sadness.

The last sound Jeremy heard was his mother saying, as she left his room after fussing with a few things, "Concussions really take it out of you, don't they"—but he didn't know whether she really said it or he'd just thought it. Then he dreamed that the young doctor at the hospital was saying it, with a red glint in his eyes.

"No," Jeremy answered, pulling his wrist away as the doctor tried to take his pulse. "The Dragon's gone. You don't have to do that."

"We've got to be careful," the doctor warned, with a grin that became a snarl, framing sharp canine teeth. "You may think it's gone, but look at the x-ray!"

Jeremy followed the doctor's pointing finger to the front-facing picture of his skull, white with gray shadow. Just look-ing at it, he shuddered, for like most people he didn't want to be reminded of the fragile stuff he was made of.

"Now watch with the ultraviolet light," the doctor coached as he turned on a small, snake-necked UV lamp and tilted it toward the x-ray. For a moment, Jeremy saw nothing special.

Then, as in a trick picture in which a hidden pattern sud-denly leaps out, he saw the bright silhouette of a dragon, tail coiled around his spinal cord, body snaking around the back of his head, and forepaws planted against the insides of his temples. From his skull's vacant sockets stared the creature's glowing eyes.

"You see," the doctor snickered, "you can never get rid of it, because it lives inside you."

"No, it's not true!" Jeremy screamed. "I'll wake up and it will be gone!"

He did wake up then, or thought he did, squeezing his eyes tight shut to stop seeing, but the image of the dragon seemed printed on the insides of his eyelids. He groaned, and then smiled with surprise to feel a soft touch on his wrist and a familiar prickle of claws.

"Cleo!" he whispered, "you're here! I was sure you were dead and I had this horrible bad dream!"

"Silly boy," she purred. "Don't you remember Alaikin telling you about the healing fluid of the crystal bees? Hr-r-mm. You humans are ver-r-ry good at petting, but cats are better at dodging dragons—and boxes."

"*Ordúrrg-Zaikh* is back, Cleo, behind my eyes. That can't be, can it?"

Cleo only purred harder, a long, resonant rumble. She sat on the side of the bed with her tail wrapped neatly around her and gazed into his eyes. He felt as if she were looking right through him, and could certainly have seen anything in there. But she simply went on purring. And then he really woke up.

Jeremy stared at the spot where Cleo had sat in his dream and listened to the hum of a distant lawnmower. He kept trying to figure out who might have given her healing balm from a crystal bee, and wishing she'd come back again, when Alaikin's melody began.

The Spider dangled above the bed, just as when it had first come. That was only two days ago, Jeremy thought, but seemed like two months. No, it seemed as if he'd always known Alaikin.

"Good show, Jeremy," the Arkanian sang. "*Ordúrrg-Zaikh* sent packing, everybody safe, and you only a headache the worse."

"Then the Dragon really is gone?" Jeremy whispered. "I had this awful nightmare that it was back and, Alaikin, it was inside my head! You could see it only with a special light, but it was there."

"I must tell you, Jeremy," Alaikin answered with a solemn melody, "that your dream was true. *Ordúrrg-Zaikh* is there, inside you, inside all of us, as it is everywhere in our universe.

The Great Dragon is the source energy of everything, the charge that powers all the worlds and the life upon them.

Without it, all would run down and stop: we would dissolve into nothingness, and the suns and their planets would fade away."

"Wait," Jeremy nearly shouted, horrified, "how can that be? *Ordúrrg-Zaikh* is pure evil! I know that, I've seen what it can do. I've felt it. And it killed Cleo! She's not here anymore—I only dreamed her."

"Cleo, dead?" Alaikin responded in a puzzled tone. "I would have sensed that, usually. Perhaps she is simply otherwise engaged. But even if she did give her life in the great struggle, you must accept the true nature of the Dragon, Jeremy. It is not pure evil, but pure energy, the Dark Energy, as your scientists call it.

"The Dragon becomes evil only in a Time of Unbalance, when it overwhelms the Light Energy that structures and guides it. Then the worlds slide toward chaos. But the damage is never final because the *Ouyperkain* restore the Balance, often at heavy cost to themselves. The Guardians, like your grandfather and now you in turn, are the true heroes of this universe.

"The cosmos thanks you, Jeremy Taylor, even unknowing what you've achieved. You felt, as rage and hate, the Dragon power unbalanced, acting to dominate everything else. But you turned to the Light Energy within you, your impulse to love, and led the Dark Energy toward good.

"In your own small world, you chose to love and help rather than hate and destroy. This is the bravest choice any being can make, the one that, if enough people make it, resets the Balance in the larger world. You have done mischief in your life and may again, but never question your courage to love and heal, for you've proven, even to your doubting self, that you have it."

Jeremy swelled with pride, but felt alongside this elation a sharp pinch of remorse. He remembered how he'd hurt people, especially Sara, when he felt hateful or jealous, how often he thought only of winning, of helping himself, before realizing how much more he would gain from loving and helping others. "I still wish *Ordúrrg-Zaikh* could be defeated once and for all, and never come back," he thought. "Life would be so much easier."

"Are you sure you want that?" Alaikin replied, its music shifting to a new key.

"If your wish should come to be,
Think upon the penalty!
Whatever in the worlds may come
Under the stars, beneath the suns,

Whether it be pain or joy,
This truth will never alter:
Storm and calm will come and go,
But neither last forever.

This refrain you'll come to know:
The worlds must keep on spinning,
Life forever losing, winning,
Or everything would disappear.

Dark and Light must wax and wane
Or the worlds will not remain.
The battle forever begun
Can never be lost and never won.

"You see," Alaikin continued somberly, "if Dragon Dark withdrew for good, so would Arkanian Light. You and all you love would fade from life. No more Jeremy, no more Alaikin, no more anything."

"Oh," Jeremy thought. "I wouldn't want that at all."

"Now you know what you must," Alaikin replied, "and I am for Arkania bound. We may meet another round. Farewell and fare thee well, Jeremy Taylor of Earth, *Brýle-Ouyperkai*, perhaps, to come."

"Can't you stay a little longer?" Jeremy whispered.

But the Arkanian's parting music already had begun. Low and flute-like, the tune, somehow both sad and joyful, played on for a few seconds until Alaikin and the silvery web faded from sight.

Jeremy was left in silence. The curtains of his room were closed to keep out brightness that might aggravate his headache, but some light still filtered through. For a while, he watched dust motes floating in its soft bright bars, and then he studied the empty white ceiling, but soon he got bored and began to drift off.

Just as his eyelids were closing, from the corner of his right eye, he thought he saw the silhouette of a cat sitting on his window sill. But as he turned his head to check, it disappeared.

I must have been dreaming again, he told himself sadly. Then he fell asleep and truly dreamed, as when he lay in the *Zhystrém Haistrál*, wild and brave visions that he might, or might not, remember when he awoke.

A PRIMAL TONGUE GLOSSARY
AND PRONUNCIATION

Alaikin (a-like'-in) – The Golden Spider, Spider

anhörin (an-hair'-in) – an Arkanian life form

Arkania (ar-cane'-nee-uh) – the planet of Alaikin

Arkanian (ar-cane'-nee-en) – One of millions of life forms on planet Arkania, all sharing the same consciousness

baibaidínn (by-by-din') – An Arkanian talker-bird, not to be mistaken for a parrot

Brŷle-Ouyperkai (bree'-lay-we'-pur-kī) – A Great Guardian

Caern Isaeth (cairn I-sayth') –The Spell of Isis

Cheihn-dürge (chine-dearj) –The Arkanian Life-storm

Dimshen-cardác (deem'-shin car-dack') – Travel-on, the Arkanian mode of long-distance travel beyond Space and Time

kailáeria (kī-lair'-ee-uh) – A Sensitive, sensing yet not possessed by Dragon Spawn

meli (may-lee) – Arkanian honey-colored furry, short form

meilixchróumistrai (may-leash-crew'-mees-try) – Arkanian honey-colored furries, long form

Ouyperkai (we'-pur-kī [rhymes with "eye"]) – A Guardian

Ouyperkain (we'-pur-cane) – Guardians

Ouyperkain Orthein (we'-pur-cane or'-thain) – the Guardians of Earth

Ordúrrg-Zaikh (or-durrg'-zike, with the rr trilled as in Spanish) – The Great Dragon

Ordúrrg-Zaikh-Ka (or-durrg'-zike kah [rhymes with "ah"] – A smaller replica of the Great Dragon that shares its power and does its bidding

shaernourddhí (share-ner-dee′) – Migration of life-essence between Arkanian life forms

Shaiféir al Shehn (shy-fear′ all shane) – *The Book of Life*

Tyrdd-cayzh (tiered-kayzh′ ["ayzh" sounds like the first part of "Asian"]) – Time-crunch, playback of compressed time and Space, which happens when exiting Dimshen-cardác

Zaik-Ka (zike kah [rhymes with "ah"]) – Short version of Ordúrrg-Zaikh-Ka (see above)

Zaikthréem (zike-threem′) – Dragon Spawn

Zhystrém Haistrál (zhee-strame′ hī-stral′ [the "zh" sounds like the "sion" in vision) – The Flowering Crystal

ABOUT THE AUTHOR

Dan Liberthson was born in Rochester, NY and attended Northwestern University (BA, history) and SUNY at Buffalo (PhD, English). In addition to *The Golden Spider*, his first children's book, he has published three illustrated books of poetry for adults, which are described on his website, **liberthson.com**. The poems in *Animal Songs* (2010) delve into the potent presence of animals in our lives. Intimates in our homes, predators or prey in the wild, and inspirations in both worlds, they help us realize what it means to be alive. Other books include *The Pitch is On the Way: Poems About Baseball and Life* (2008), which explores baseball and what the game means to its fans, and *A Family Album* (2006), poems about his childhood in and growth out of an American Jewish family with a mentally ill sister.

CPSIA information can be obtained
at www.ICGtesting.com
Printed in the USA
FSOW02n0725270917
39237FS